Wheel of the Moon

Wheel of the Moon

SANDRA FORRESTER

HarperCollinsPublishers

Wheel of the Moon
Copyright © 2000 by Sandra Forrester
All rights reserved. No part of this book may be used or reproduced in any manner
whatsoever without written permission except in the case of brief quotations
embodied in critical articles and reviews. Printed in the United States of America.
For information address HarperCollins Children's Books, a division of
HarperCollins Publishers, 1350 Avenue of the Americas, New York, NY 10019.
www.harperchildrens.com

Library of Congress Cataloging-in-Publication Data
Forrester, Sandra.
  Wheel of the Moon / Sandra Forrester.
    p.   cm.
  Summary: In England in 1627, newly orphaned Pen Downing leaves her
country village for London, where she is abducted and sent to Virginia to work
as an indentured servant.
  ISBN 0-688-17149-4 (trade)—ISBN 0-06-029203-2 (library)
  [1. Orphans—Fiction.   2. Indentured servants—Fiction.   3. Great Britain—
History—17th century—Fiction.   4.Virginia—History—Colonial period,
1600–1775—Fiction.]   I. Title.
PZ7.F7717 Wh   2000
[Fic]—dc21   99-87804
                                                                         CIP
                                                                          AC

Typography by Hilary Zarycky
1   2   3   4   5   6   7   8   9   10
❖
First Edition

To Barbara Kouts and Rosemary Brosnan—
with gratitude to my guardian angel
for finding you both

April 1627
England

1

WHEN PEN OPENED HER eyes, the purple-gray sky was edged with gold. The room smelled of wood smoke and the dried herbs hanging from the rafters. Pen's mother was kneading dough and shaping it into farthing and halfpenny loaves.

"Fair morn, Mistress Lazybones," her mother said. "Will you be seeing to the goats, or is it your plan to lie abed all day?"

Pen laughed and sprang up from her pallet. On the way to the privy, she kissed her mother on the cheek and raced for the door before Mam could swat her backside.

The goats waited impatiently in their pen. Maud was black and Emma was brown, with white spots. They bleated and danced around Pen's feet as she brought the milk pails. Emma butted Pen's legs gently and buried her soft face in Pen's hand.

Pen had nearly finished the milking when she saw the village girls taking their animals to the high meadow. The girls talked and laughed as they crossed the ravine behind the cottage and started up the cliff to the grazing land. They pretended not to see her, but Pen knew they watched her from the corners of their eyes. When they passed her in the village, they glanced away so they wouldn't have to speak.

Their mothers did the same with Mam, but Pen's mother walked through the village with a proud stride. She didn't seem to notice the villagers' whispers and cunning looks. Pen knew that Mam's refusal to bow her head in shame grated on them.

Like her mother, Pen would not humble herself before the village, but she heard what the neighbors whispered. They said it was good that Judith Downing's mother and father hadn't lived to see what she'd come to. They called it a blessing that her parents weren't here to know about their bastard grandchild. Mam said that Roger Banks would have married her; there just wasn't time.

Mam didn't speak often of Pen's father. All Pen knew of him were the bits and pieces of memory her mother chose to share in odd moments. He grew up with Mam in this village, but her mother said he had always dreamed of far-off places. Mam knew early on that she loved him, following him about from the time she was a young girl. It took him longer to realize he loved her, as well. One day, when Mam was fourteen, the same age as Pen was now, Roger Banks said, "I would marry you, but I can't stay and work the land until I die. I want more than that." Soon after, he left for London in search of more. Pen thought her mother would have been too proud to follow if she hadn't known a babe was on the way.

The girls were far enough away now for Pen to watch them straight on. They had started up the side of the cliff and the climb was hard. Spring rains had turned the track to mud. The sheep and goats were surefooted, but the girls slipped and slid on the oozing ground as it turned sharply upward. A strong wind grabbed at their skirts and whipped their hair, but they didn't seem to mind. Their laughter was carried back to Pen on the wind.

Pen watched and strained to catch their words. They had never asked her to go with them to the high meadow, so she wondered what they talked about, what made them laugh.

"Finished with the milking?"

Pen hadn't noticed her mother leave the cottage, and the voice startled her. Mam took the pails from Pen, but she didn't go back inside. They stood together, watching the girls.

Finally, Mam said, "When the bread's done, I'll go with you to take the goats."

"You needn't," Pen said sharply.

"Seems a fine day to climb to the meadow," Mam said, and started inside with the milk.

Pen went to the well for water and swept the floor clean before they set out. The girls had long since left their animals to graze and come back to the village.

Maud and Emma were frisky as they set off through the ravine. It was a deep cavern with rocky sides, carved out by ancient waters but dry now except when the rains came.

The nannies' hooves clicked against the stones, becoming muffled thuds when they reached the dirt path that wound up the cliff. The track was pocked with animal prints, and the air smelled of fresh droppings. High above them, a bit of blue sky peeked through the jagged rocks that rose to meet it.

The goats tripped eagerly up the path, knowing that new spring grass awaited them, and Mam followed close behind. Pen came more slowly, her feet caked to the ankle with mud and dung.

When they finally reached the top, Pen and her mother were breathing hard. But while Pen sank to the ground to rest, Mam followed Maud and Emma into the grazing land.

The meadow was a pool of silver-green, the tall grass rippling and bowing in the wind. It smelled of wet earth and rosemary.

Mam had taken off her cap. Her long hair had come loose from its pins and blew around her face. How young she looks, Pen thought, how filled with pure pleasure. It had been a year or more since her mother had left her chores to walk in the meadow.

Pen had her mother's dark hair, but Judith's eyes were as blue as the forget-me-nots that would soon bloom outside their door. Pen's eyes were greenish gray, like her father's.

Mam had said that she and Pen's father used to walk in the meadow together. That was before he left for London. Before Mam followed him there. He joined a group of players, Mam said, and acted on the stage. They gave him small parts—that of soldier, peasant, groom—and sometimes a line to speak.

He was glad to see her, Mam said, and happier still to learn a child was on the way. But his joy was short-lived, for soon Pen's mother took ill and he hadn't the money to care for her. He was caught making off with a bit of beef from the butcher and thrown into the gaol. That was where he died, three months before his daughter was born.

The villagers said Roger Banks was good for nothing. They called him scoundrel and thief. But Mam said that he had been gentle and kind, that he had brightened the earth with his presence.

Pen watched her mother lift her face to the sun. Then Mam turned to Pen, smiling.

They walked hand in hand through the grass. It was like being at the top of the world, alone but for the sheep and goats and singing birds. They waded into the rippling pool of the meadow, and they laughed.

Pen and her mother worked late into the night, making up for time lost in the meadow. There was tomorrow's stew to put on the fire, the goats to tend, and Mam's cart to load with bread. Before first light, she would begin the long journey to London Town to sell her loaves and the little goat cheese they could spare.

The moon was high when they finally came inside to bed. Mam moved slowly, shoulders hunched, rubbing an ache in her back.

"I could go with you," Pen said as she settled under

her blanket. "I could help pull the cart."

Mam blew out the candle nub. "Tomorrow you must plant," she said.

"I've only seen London twice," Pen said. Her voice was sulky.

"Next time, mayhap."

Pen turned away in disappointment and saw the moon framed by the window. Mam watched the wheel of the moon as it passed through the seasons to foretell of rain or snow, to know when to plant and when to gather honey for mead.

"There's a ring around the moon," Pen said.

Mam was still, and Pen knew she was looking out the window.

"Rain tomorrow," Mam said.

"If it rains, the roads will turn to mud," Pen said hopefully. "You'll need me to pull the cart."

"I'll need you to plant," Mam said firmly.

One day, Pen thought, I will go to London. I'll leave this village and the laughing girls and never come back. Pen pictured the streets of London as she remembered them, crammed with carts and carriages and people and noise. More excitement in a day than these villagers would know in a lifetime. She thought of the boys and old men sitting on the banks of the great River Thames with their lines in the water.

"I'll go to London one day," she said to Mam, "and make me living selling fish to the fishmongers."

"Will you, now?" Mam asked in a tired voice, and lay down on her pallet.

8

Pen waited for Mam to say that life in London was too hard. That she couldn't bear to see Pen go. But Mam turned over on her side, already losing herself in sleep, and said no more.

Pen watched the moon until it rose beyond the window frame. The black, empty sky filled her with sadness. She closed her eyes and thought how it would be to leave this cottage for the last time. Her mother would walk with her as far as the road. And Mam would stand there, her eyes fixed on the road to London Town, long after Pen was out of sight.

2

PEN MILKED THE GOATS while Mam made tea and warmed up porridge from the day before. The sky was still dark when they finished breakfast.

Mam brought out pouches of seeds. "If the rain comes, you needn't water after you plant," she said.

Pen was still sulking because Mam was leaving her behind. She nodded but said nothing.

"Heat up the stew when you get hungry," Mam said. "There's a fresh loaf in the cupboard."

Pen nodded again, noticing for the first time how the candlelight cast shadows beneath her mother's eyes and showed up the furrows in her brow. Mam still looked weary after a full night's rest, and suddenly Pen was ashamed of her ill humor.

"Don't worry about the planting," Pen said quickly. "I'll take care to do it as you would."

"I know you will," Mam said.

Mam draped her old cloak around her shoulders and gathered up the bread and smoked fish she would eat midday. Pen followed her to the door, wishing she had not been cross.

"Will you be home before dark?" Pen asked.

"It all depends on how they buy," Mam said.

"I'll have hot stew waiting."

A smile lifted the corners of Mam's mouth, and she didn't look so tired. Her hand brushed Pen's cheek, and then she was gone.

Pen took the goats to the meadow and was back before the other girls had finished their milking. The sun was still low when she started planting: dill, soapwort, meadowsweet, chamomile. She made her way slowly down the furrows, pushing one seed at a time into the soft earth. The sun climbed high and her hair grew damp under her cap, but she scarcely noticed. She didn't stop until all the seeds were planted.

Standing up and stretching to ease the ache in her back, Pen was surprised to see great black clouds rolling in from beyond the cliff. The sun was hidden somewhere behind them.

She ate a little of the stew before starting the chores inside. The afternoon passed quickly as she moved from cleaning the hearth to sweeping the floor to churning the goats' milk into butter. She was feeling pleased with herself, and with the day's work, when the storm moved in. The rain came hard, all at once, soaking the thatched roof and running off in streams through the garden. Pen looked out the door and all she could see was blowing rain.

It worried her that Mam might be caught on the road in this. Then she thought of the goats. Bringing them down the cliff in a storm wouldn't be easy, and the longer she waited, the harder it would be. She covered her head with a shawl and started for the meadow.

The rain struck her face like slaps of a hand. She found her way blindly down the slope behind the cottage from memory and from the feel of the earth beneath her feet.

Water was standing ankle-deep in the cavern floor. Pen felt a twinge of alarm. If she didn't bring the goats down quickly, they might all be spending the night in the meadow.

Pen started up the path and slipped, landing hard on her hands. When she tried to stand, she fell again. Only by grabbing an outcrop of rock could she pull herself upright.

The storm was terrible, and Pen wondered if she should turn back. But Mam would expect her to care for the goats, no matter what. How would they make it through the winter without milk and cheese and butter?

At times, Pen was forced to crawl on her hands and knees. She was soaked and shivering with cold. Her palms stung where the sharp stones had cut them, and her fingers were numb from grasping the rocks. She thought how easy it would be to let go and slide in the mud to the bottom. "I tried," she could tell Mam. But Pen could imagine Mam's worry over the goats, so she gripped the rocks tighter and continued on.

The wind came in gusts now and pushed her this way

and that. Such a mournful sound it made as it blew around the cliff.

It had grown dark. Pen didn't know how far she was from the meadow, and she was afraid. Her back and shoulders throbbing, she sat down to decide what to do next. She could keep climbing—and pray the wind didn't sweep her to her death—or she could stay where she was and wait for the storm to pass.

As she considered her choices, Pen heard a faint cry overhead. Close by, it seemed, though it was hard to tell over the wailing of the wind. Pen sat very still, listening.

Aye, it was goats bleating. She must be close to the top.

Hope and excitement gave Pen new strength. She started to climb again. The cries grew louder.

Pen stopped to call the goats' names. A shower of pebbles fell, bouncing off the rocks and striking her hands and arms. Then something heavy slid into her legs, nearly causing her to tumble backward.

Pen crouched and felt wet fur beneath her fingers. The animal struggled to stand. Then a small face slipped into Pen's hand and she knew that she had found Emma.

Since the goats never strayed far from each other, Pen called Maud's name. She was answered by a piteous cry. Pen held firmly to Emma and coaxed Maud to her with encouraging words.

They began the journey down. Pen couldn't see the goats in the darkness, but she could hear them kick up loose stones and scramble to keep their footing on the path. She thought of Mam and wondered if she was at home, waiting. Home. It seemed very far away.

With every step, Pen worried that they might plunge over the rocks into the ravine. She was aware of nothing but the darkness, the cold, the howling wind—the fear.

Pen lost track of time. She had no idea where they were, and she was surprised when the path began to level off. Pen let out a sigh of relief. They had made it down the cliff and were nearly home. She moved quickly now, picturing Mam's glad face when she saw Pen with the goats.

Pen was so eager to be home, she forgot to be cautious. She didn't hear the roaring water until it was too late—until she stepped into the icy flow and the earth fell away.

The cavern was flooded. The current seized her and pulled her under.

Pen tried to kick to the surface, but her body was numb with cold and exhaustion. She couldn't feel her arms and legs. Her chest close to bursting, Pen thought, We will die here. But then her head broke through the water's surface. Coughing and sputtering, she screamed for help.

Above the terrible roar, she heard a voice.

Aye, it was her name the voice was calling. She wasn't dreaming this. It was her mother's voice, shouting, "Pen! Hold on!"

The water dragged Pen under again. She was too weary to fight it.

Pen opened her eyes to a light so bright, it blinded her. She twisted her head away and clenched her eyes shut.

"Move the torch," a man said.

Pen heard a murmur of voices. Her head was swimming and her chest felt raw when she tried to breathe. Suddenly, her mouth filled with water and she thought she was going to be sick. She tried to sit up, but someone pushed her back roughly. She spat out the water; some of Mam's stew came with it.

She heard a woman's voice. For an instant, Pen thought it was her mother's, but the voice was too harsh to be Mam's.

Pen opened her eyes again. Blurred faces stared down at her. Pen squinted to bring them into focus, searching for her mother. But Mam's face wasn't among them.

A woman said, "You'd best tell her, Preacher."

It was the Reverend Howard's face that moved close to Pen's, so close that she could see the blackened nubs of teeth as his lips parted. "Your mother's dead," he said. "Swept off by the water, and she couldn't be saved."

Pen blinked and turned her face away. She thought she was going to be sick again.

"Did she hear?"

"Does she understand what he said?"

Their whispers angered Pen. She understood what the preacher had said, but he was wrong. She had heard Mam calling. Pen was just too weak to argue.

"The goats," she said hoarsely.

"They're safe," someone answered.

It looked as though the whole village had gathered on the rise behind their cottage—everyone except Mam.

15

Pen fought the grogginess that threatened to swallow her. She *must* stay awake. She must *think*! If Mam were alive, Pen reasoned, she would be here, scolding Pen for taking such risks, then pulling her close. But Mam wasn't here.

That was when Pen knew her mother was dead.

The old woman Sarah Alwin grabbed Pen's arm and said, "You'll stay with us."

Pen closed her eyes to the staring faces. It didn't matter what they said or what they did with her. She didn't resist when Sarah and Hugh Alwin pulled her up and led her away.

They took her to the goat shed behind their cottage. Hugh Alwin held up his lantern and pointed to a pile of straw in the shed where goats were huddled.

"You can sleep there," he said gruffly.

Pen looked at the goats. Hugh Alwin's old white nanny was there, and Emma and Maud, wet and shivering with cold.

Pen moved toward them—so glad to see Emma and Maud alive—then stopped. Why are they here in this shed? she wondered. But her thinking wasn't clear enough to puzzle it out.

Sarah Alwin brought a ragged blanket. "Cover up with this," she said.

The blanket was scratchy wool and stank worse than the goats.

"I'll sleep in me own cottage," Pen said, and turned to go. Tomorrow, she thought groggily, tomorrow I'll come back for Emma and Maud.

Hugh Alwin was an old man, but his grip was painful on her arm. "It's not your cottage now," he said. "They'll give it to whoever can pay the rent."

"*I* can pay the rent!" Pen cried.

"Nay," Sarah Alwin said. "They'll not give the cottage to a girl."

Pen felt a rush of panic, for she knew what they said was true. She was an orphan now, and not entitled to anything of her own. Everything that was Mam's would go to whoever took Pen in, as payment for her keep.

Hugh Alwin pushed her into the shed and shut the door. Pen heard him lower the bar and realized with shock that he had locked her in.

She stood in the darkness for a moment, not knowing what to do. Her thoughts were jumbled. Nothing that had happened this night seemed real.

Sinking to the ground, Pen crawled through the straw to Emma and Maud. The goats pressed against her side, their bodies warming her and providing a measure of comfort.

"I must take one thought at a time," Pen said slowly, "and try to make sense of it."

But she couldn't grasp it all at once—that everything was gone.

Mam. The cottage. Everything.

Gone.

3

PEN LAY IN THE straw all night, thinking, not sleeping. At times, she saw Mam's face in the darkness and it seemed so real, Pen thought she must have dreamed that Mam was gone. Feeling giddy with relief and joy, she imagined waking up in the cottage. Mam would be there and the terrible dream would be over.

But then the truth would hit hard, leaving her weak and aching with the horror of it, and she'd know this wasn't a dream.

Mam was dead.

Pen had seen death before. Many times. Old men and women too worn-out to go on. Babies too weak to begin. Even folks in their prime falling prey to sickness. But Mam wasn't old or weak or ill. How could her laughter be stilled so suddenly? How could that bright spark of life be doused forever? *How?*

Hugh Alwin opened the door to the shed at dawn and handed Pen a bit of hard bread.

"Eat," he said. "Then milk the goats and muck out the shed."

"I want to see me mother," Pen said.

"In time," he responded, and walked away.

Pen was cleaning the shed when the preacher came. She smelled of sour goat. Her dress was still wet and clung to her legs. The Reverend Howard studied her with disapproving eyes.

"Judith Downing will have a proper burial, with shroud and ale," he said. "You'll work off the cost."

Aye, Pen thought, her mother deserved a decent burial.

"It's agreed you'll stay with Goodman Alwin and his wife," the Reverend Howard went on. "They're God-fearing people not able to do for themselves. They can use a young back."

Pen said nothing. I will pay for Mam's burial, she thought. Then she would see.

Sarah Alwin kept her running all day, but Pen found time to bring water to the goats. When she saw the pail, Sarah Alwin said, "I didn't tell you to go to the well," and backhanded Pen across the face.

Goody Alwin is strong, Pen thought, for someone not able to do for herself.

Late that day, Sarah Alwin came to Pen and said, "You'll pay your respects to Judith Downing."

She handed Pen a black shawl. The wool was soft and smelled of lavender. It was Mam's shawl. Sarah Alwin was wearing Mam's best dress and linen cap.

"Cover your head," Goody Alwin said.

Pen draped the shawl over her hair and followed the old woman down the road to Alice Beal's cottage. Goodwife Beal met them at the door. She looked almost pitying as she led Pen to her mother.

Mam lay on a table against the wall. The only light came from candles burning at her head and feet. Their flames cowered in the draft Pen made as she walked to the table, leaving her mother's face in shadow. Pen felt the numbness of disbelief as she looked into that face.

Mam seemed to be sleeping. Death had smoothed the furrows from her brow and she looked peaceful. Mam was beyond caring that her child was left to go on without her.

Pen reeled inwardly as she began to realize the unthinkable—that she was alone. Completely and forever alone. Even as the realization struck her, she tried to deny it. Even as she stared into her mother's lifeless face, she grasped for a sliver of hope, a way to turn back time. If only I hadn't gone after the goats, Pen thought. If I'd gone home when I saw how bad it was. And that was when the most unbearable truth hit—that she had caused her mother's death. Mam would be alive if she hadn't gone in search of her daughter.

Pen gripped the edge of the table to steady herself, brushing against Mam's sleeve. She noticed that Alice Beal had placed a white cap on Mam's head and dressed her in someone's old gown. The cloth was faded and worn at the neck.

Pen wanted to cry out to Sarah Alwin, *Why should my mother be buried in this while you wear her best gown?* But she said nothing. What did it matter now?

Pen touched Mam's hand. It was cold and unyielding. The chill spread through Pen's body and she began to tremble.

Alice Beal came to stand with her. "The burial's tomorrow," she said.

Pen nodded. She knew she should thank the woman for tending Mam, but the words wouldn't come.

The women wrapped Judith Downing in a piece of white cloth and tied it with heavy cord. The men lifted her into a plank box.

Everyone in the village had gathered to follow the coffin to the churchyard. Alice Beal gave the mourners sprigs of rosemary. She handed out bread and cheese and ale. The villagers took the food and drink greedily.

Pen walked behind the coffin, with Hugh Alwin on one side, Sarah on the other. Goodman Alwin finished his bread and cheese before they were halfway through the village.

The villagers' faces were somber, but there was an eagerness about them. They care nothing that my mother is dead, Pen thought. This was a holiday, a reason to stay in from the fields, with free food and ale, besides.

The sun was so bright, it hurt Pen's eyes. It should be as dark and dismal as the night Mam died, Pen thought. That would be only right.

The preacher waited at the edge of the churchyard. He looked on solemnly as the men carried the coffin through the gate.

The graves were shaded by chestnut trees. Pen expected the men to stop where Mam's mother and father were buried, but they walked past all the graves and beyond the trees to a barren field on the north side of the churchyard. They lowered the coffin to the ground beside a freshly dug hole.

The Reverend Howard came to stand beside the hole, and the villagers gathered around him. Some were still eating and drinking. Pen hadn't touched her food or ale, and Hugh Alwin eyed it hungrily.

Pen understood now. The villagers were keeping her mother apart in death as they had in life, burying her away from her family and theirs. She would be alone, save for the bones of Mim Bailey, a suicide. This field was the burial place of sinners.

The Reverend Howard began to speak, but Pen shut out his voice. He hadn't known her mother, so how could his words have anything to do with Mam?

When the preacher had finished, the men lifted Judith Downing's shrouded body from the box and lowered it into the hole. They would take the coffin back to the village to use for the next burial.

Sarah Alwin nudged Pen toward the grave. The old woman dropped her rosemary into the hole and waited for Pen to do the same.

Pen thought of Mam wearing the cast-off gown. She

thought of the women turning their heads when Mam walked past. Her mother wouldn't want their offerings, Pen decided, and flung the rosemary into the field.

The villagers gasped and whispered among themselves. Sarah Alwin's eyes glittered with anger.

They hurried Pen from the churchyard and back to the goat shed. When Hugh Alwin was certain that no one could see, he took a strap to Pen until the blood flowed down her back.

Later, lying in the straw with the goats, Pen whimpered softly. But the bitterness swelling inside her was stronger than any physical pain.

She would not cry.

Every day was the same. Hugh Alwin woke Pen before first light, gave her a bit of bread, and put her to work. She plowed their fields and cared for their animals, cooked their food and cleaned their cottage. Sometimes they loaned her out to Goodwife Beal, as payment for the burial food and shroud. At day's end, they gave her more bread and sent her to sleep with the goats.

But they no longer locked the shed.

Since Mam was gone, the whispers had changed. Now the villagers said that Pen—Judith Downing's bastard—should be grateful that someone would take her in. They said that Hugh Alwin and his wife were rich with three goats. Aye, Pen thought, they could save the goats, but not my mother. The goats were worth something to them.

Pen heard, too, that one of the laughing girls was to be wed. She would marry Giles, the miller's son. The villagers said she'd done well to snare Giles, and lucky they were to have a cottage waiting. Pen didn't have to guess which cottage. There was only one in the village that stood empty.

After a time, Pen considered her debt to the village paid. When she gathered up the bedding to air, she took her mother's shawl, cap, and best dress without Sarah Alwin knowing and hid them in the goat shed. She would leave that night before the old woman found them missing.

The moon was high and the village slept when Pen opened the door to the shed and brought out Maud and Emma. They followed her willingly across the croft to the road.

Hugging Mam's things to her chest, Pen went first to the churchyard. She sat down on the earth that covered Mam and began to talk. She spoke to her mother for such a long time, the goats grew restless and wandered into the churchyard in search of grass.

Pen asked Mam for her blessing. The whisper she heard could have been the wind blowing through the trees.

Pen walked on. It was nearly dawn when she came to another village. She saw a herd of goats fenced in at one of the cottages. Pen opened the gate, and Maud and Emma trotted in to join the others.

How surprised someone will be to find two new

goats, Pen thought as she walked back to the road. She wished she could take Maud and Emma with her. But at least they were free of Hugh and Sarah Alwin. She owed them that.

May 1627
London

4

Pen saw the church spires first, rising so high into the sky, they seemed to pierce the clouds. Then she noticed coal smoke billowing from hundreds of blackened chimneys. Her legs ached and her belly rumbled, but this first sight of the city banished all thoughts of weariness and hunger. She could only gawk and marvel as the road turned to cobbled streets and she found herself swallowed up by the noise and confusion of London.

The streets were clogged with carts and carriages and people. Gentlemen tipped their hats to one another and stepped around the drunks and beggars sprawled in the gutters. Ragged children played in doorways. Babies crawled in the dirt. Women swept their doorsteps and threw buckets of slop out the windows. Soot from the chimneys rained down like dirty snow, turning everything gray.

London smelled of fish and boiling tar and rotting garbage. And the noise! Wheels clattered over the cobbles, bells rang, and women cried out, "Oysters! Oysters!" and "Hot buns for a penny!"

Pen had forgotten how big London was. How the streets twisted and turned and lost themselves in dark nooks and crannies. Mam had known which streets to follow to the market on Cheapside. She had known how to push through the tangle of bodies and hold tight to her purse.

Pen knew none of this. She knew only that she was somewhere in London, alone.

She gripped Mam's things and looked around for a face that seemed kind, for someone to ask how to get to Cheapside. She knew people at the market and hoped they would remember her, as well. The old woman called Nellie, with her basket of pins and ribbons. Blind Bess, who sold fruits and vegetables. Mayhap they would have a bit of food to spare and could tell her how to make her way in the city.

But the people hurrying past had hard faces. They pushed and shoved and knocked Pen aside without seeming to notice she was there. Except for a man in a fine coat who shouted, "Out of my way, beggar!" and struck her with his walking stick.

Pen staggered back, her arm smarting, and fell into the street. She just had time to leap out of the way before a carriage bore down on her.

Pen heard laughter and turned to see a gang of boys watching her, smirking. They started toward her, looking up to no good, and she ran.

Now Pen was the one shoving bodies aside. A woman in full skirts cursed her. A man unloading hogsheads of ale lifted his hand as though to cuff her and snarled.

Pen darted into a narrow street and ran the length of it, dodging people as best she could. She turned into an alley and ducked behind a pile of broken crates. Only then did she look back, expecting to see the boys racing after her. But the alley was empty.

Pen crouched behind the crates to catch her breath and to think. She was hungry, and if she was to make a living selling fish, she'd need a hook and line. But she had no money and nothing to sell. Only Mam's gown, cap, and shawl.

When Pen crept out from her hiding place, she searched the busy street for the boys. They were no-where in sight. Having grown somewhat accustomed to the noise and press of bodies, she entered the bustle less fearfully.

Pen thought of Mam hawking her bread and cheese, and she made her decision. "Shawl for sale!" Pen cried out to passersby. "Fine soft wool! Shawl for a shilling!"

Sometimes her cries drew a glance from one of the hard faces. But once they saw what she was selling, their eyes darted away and they hurried on.

As the day passed, Pen's belly rumbled louder and her legs began to tremble with exhaustion. It seemed that she had walked most of the streets of London and still hadn't sold the shawl, nor was she any closer to finding Cheapside.

The smell of the river with its fish and sewage was

strong. The sky was speckled with gulls that swooped and shrieked and littered the cobblestones with their droppings. There were few women in this part of the city, and the ones who were there looked old and ragged and spent.

Then Pen noticed the girl.

She wasn't much older than Pen, and she was uncommonly pretty, with a tangle of black curls falling to her shoulders. Her lips and cheeks were unnaturally red. She wore a frilled bonnet and a fine black gown with crimson petticoats trimmed in silver lace. The lace was torn and the skirt's hem was stained with filth from dragging in the street. But Pen had never seen such a gown before and couldn't help staring.

As though sensing someone's eyes on her, the girl turned to look at Pen. She studied Pen thoughtfully for a moment, then started toward her.

The girl's painted lips curved into a smile as she approached. Her dark eyes glittered with life and cunning. "What have you here, Mistress Mouse?" she said cheerfully, and reached out to touch the shawl. Her hands were black with grime. "Is it rags you're peddling?"

Pen jerked Mam's shawl away. "It's a fine shawl I'm selling," she retorted. "The softest wool in all of England."

"Is it, now!" the girl exclaimed, her voice dancing with merriment. "And have you touched all the wool in England, Mistress Mouse?"

"Me *name* is Pen."

"Very well, *Pen,*" the girl said, "though Mouse suits you better. I'm called Rose."

Pen saw that the girl was laughing at her, but it wasn't cruel laughter. She felt a stirring of hope. "Could you use a shawl for these damp, cool evenings?" Pen coaxed. "It's yours for a shilling."

"Too much," Rose said. The smile faded and her eyes strayed from Pen to the crowded street. She seemed to be watching for someone. "Besides which, I've no need for a countrywoman's shawl—even if it *is* the softest wool in England."

She turned abruptly to go, and Pen panicked. It would be dark soon, and she feared being left alone. Without a plan, Pen started after her.

Rose looked back and frowned. "I've no need for the shawl," she repeated sharply. "Good day to you, Mistress Mouse. And have a care. There's them on these streets that prey on such as you."

Pen watched the girl cross the street and head for an alehouse, then stop outside the door. Pen wondered what she was waiting for.

A gentleman came out and Rose said something to him. He shook his head and brushed past her. Then Rose walked up to a man wearing a fine cloak and hat. She had scarcely opened her mouth to speak before he pushed her aside and moved on.

Pen could see the disappointment in Rose's face. But she was smiling again when another gentleman approached. He stopped and listened to what she had to say, then nodded. Pen watched as Rose trotted down the street after him.

Dusk was gathering and the street was clearing of people. Pen looked around helplessly. What am I to do now? she wondered. Where am I to go?

5

SHE SOLD THE SHAWL to a woman for two pence. It was worth more, but night was falling and the streets seemed even more menacing by lamplight than by day.

Gripping the pennies in her fist, lest some cutpurse make off with them and leave her with nothing, Pen considered what to do next. She could buy a meal and a noggin of small beer, but if she spent all her money at the alehouse, she'd have none left for the fishhook and line.

Ignoring the pangs in her belly, Pen decided to find a place to bed down for the night. On the morrow, she would ask where to buy a hook and line. And before the sun sets again, Pen thought, I will have caught enough fish to buy a week's meals.

She wandered the streets a long time before settling on a place to spend the night. At the end of an alley, she found some hogsheads stacked against a wall. She crawled behind the barrels, tucked the two pence into Mam's cap, and curled up under her mother's dress to sleep.

Lying on the hard ground, Pen remembered her own soft pallet at home. She thought of nights spent under her blanket, her belly filled with Mam's good food. She thought of Mam walking through the meadow, her dark hair whipped by the wind. Pen fell asleep to the sound of her mother's laughter.

Exhausted from her long journey, and from a day spent walking London's streets, Pen slept soundly through the night and late into the following day. When she finally woke, she couldn't remember where she was. Her first awareness was of the stench that filled her nostrils.

Pen sat up and saw an old man sprawled at her feet. His shirt and breeches were in tatters. He reeked of sour ale, vomit, and sweat.

Pen leaped to her feet. She stumbled over the man as she left her hiding place. Even the sharp nudge of her heel didn't wake him, and she wondered if he was dead. But then he let out a resounding snore. Pen hurried away before he could rouse himself and take a mind to slit her throat.

When she left the alley, Pen saw that the street was strangely clear of carts and carriages but even more crowded with people than the day before. They lined the street ten-deep, waiting for something.

A woman was there with a babe in her arms and two little ones holding to her skirts.

"Why are they gathered here?" Pen asked the woman.

"For the hanging."

"What hanging?"

"Why, a thief's to be hung," the woman said, her voice quivering with excitement.

Pen looked at the people around her. They spoke in hushed voices, at the same time craning their necks, hoping to be the first to see the condemned man brought past. For the first time, it occurred to Pen that her father had been fortunate to draw his last breath in the solitude of the gaol.

It wasn't long before they heard the clatter of wooden wheels and the tramping of horses' hooves on the cobblestones.

"He's coming," the people whispered. "They're bringing him now."

Pen meant to look away, but she found her eyes stuck fast to the man tied, standing, in the cart. Surrounding him were men on horseback, with padded doublets and shining swords. So many of them, Pen thought, to guard just one man—and a puny one at that. Terribly thin, he was, and his shirt hung in bloodied shreds where the lash had met his back. He had the thick dark hair of a young man, but he was looking down, so Pen couldn't be certain. His head bobbed limply as the cart jolted over the cobbles, and his shoulders sagged.

Pen turned away and pushed into the crowd of watchers. So intent were they on seeing the man to his hanging, they stood rooted in her path. Pen shouldered her way through, just as intent on leaving this place.

Then she felt a shove in return, and her bundle was wrenched away. A boy with red hair tucked the prize under his arm and disappeared into the swarm of bodies.

"Thief!" Pen shouted. "Stop, thief!" And she started after him.

The boy was small and easy to lose in the crowd, but his bright hair stood out. Pen lost sight of him for a moment, then spotted the russet head as it turned a corner.

Pen followed him into an alley—and stopped. The passageway ended almost before it began, with a brick wall. There was no place to hide and no exit. Yet the boy was gone. It was as if he had disappeared by magic.

Then Pen noticed a window just above the ground. It was boarded up and narrow, but large enough, she realized, for the boy to fit through.

She pulled at the boards, but they didn't move. Disgusted that the little scut had gotten away with all she had left of Mam, Pen kicked at the boards. They shifted.

She fell to her knees and pushed the planks to the side. They swung away easily. It was pitch-dark inside. When Pen stuck her head through the window, she could see nothing. The air was cool and smelled of dampness.

Dare I go in after him? Pen wondered. He was a scrawny little thing, surely not strong enough to do anyone harm. But was he alone? Could there be others bigger and stronger waiting to crack her over the head?

She decided to follow the boy. How dare he take all she had and think he could get away with it!

Pen slipped through the hole, feetfirst. She lowered herself into the darkness, holding on to the window ledge for support. Her legs dangled in midair. Suddenly, she felt the rotting wood crumble under her fingers. She struggled to pull herself up, but the wood gave way. She plummeted through the darkness.

Her feet hit the earth full force. Pain shot up her legs and they crumpled beneath her.

6

PEN RAN HER HANDS gingerly down her legs. She didn't feel any broken bones, but her ankles throbbed. She wasn't sure she could stand. And even if she could, Pen wondered where she would go. She couldn't see anything but darkness around her.

Pen touched the cold packed-earth floor. It was wet and smelled of mildew. She rose unsteadily to her knees, then to her feet. She hurt from her hips to her toes, but when she took a hesitant step, Pen found that her aching legs would bear her weight.

She reached out and felt rough brick and crumbling mortar. Inching her way along the wall, Pen brushed against cobwebs. Faint sounds of rustling and scurrying told Pen that she was disturbing the rats and whatever other creatures lived there in the dark.

She rounded a corner, and her fingers found a doorknob jutting out from the wall. She turned the knob and pushed. The door creaked but didn't move. She tried again, this time throwing her shoulder against the door. It groaned open.

Soft light flooded the doorway and Pen heard gasps of surprise.

"What the devil!" someone exclaimed. It was a man's voice.

Then a girl said sharply, "Who are you? What are you doing here?"

The girl took a step toward Pen. She was holding a candle. Pen saw a tumble of flaxen curls around a small, startled face. The face didn't seem to be one that Pen should fear. Indeed, the girl wasn't much older than Pen and had a fragile look about her.

But there were two others standing behind the girl— a young man and a boy with hair that glowed copper in the candlelight. Pen would have recognized that hair anywhere, just as surely as she knew the fabric of Mam's gown clutched to his chest. What den of thieves had she stumbled into?

The young man came to stand beside the girl. His face was wary. "Who are you, and why have you come here?" he asked.

Pen looked from him to the boy. "You stole my bundle," she said.

"It's a pickpurse I am, after all," the boy said with cheerful arrogance.

The man's head snapped toward the boy. He eyed the cloth in the boy's arms. "Give it back," he said.

The boy's face turned defiant. His fingers tightened around Mam's dress.

"Jory."

The boy dropped his head, considering. Then he

41

raised his eyes to Pen and heaved the bundle at her.

Pen unfolded Mam's dress and found the cap with the two pence knotted inside.

"Tell her you're sorry," the man said.

"You want me to lie?" Jory demanded. "And how are we to eat, with you making me give everything back?"

"Let Elinor and me worry about that," the man said. His expression was stern, but Pen thought she heard amusement behind his words.

"You bring in just enough to keep us from starving," the boy grumbled.

"No more, you scalawag," the girl said. "Go put some wood on the fire, and see if you can't stay out of mischief."

"Aye," the man said. "We don't need you leading the bailiff here."

Jory gave Pen a look of disdain before swaggering through a doorway behind him.

"We ask your pardon for Jory," the girl said to Pen. "He's too stubborn to ask for himself."

Pen didn't know what to make of these people, nor of this place that seemed more like an underground cave than a proper house.

"I'm Elinor Jarvis," the girl said. "This is me brother, Bram."

"The boy—Jory," Pen said. "Is he your brother, too?"

"Nay," Elinor said. "At least not by blood."

"Who are you?" Bram asked. He had his sister's fair hair and blue eyes. The eyes appeared less vigilant now.

"Me name's Pen Downing."

"You're not from London," Elinor said, taking in Pen's country homespun. "Are you on your own in the city?"

"Aye."

"Are your folks dead, then?" Bram asked.

Pen nodded.

"Bram and me's orphans, too," Elinor said. "Da and Mam died of the dark sickness"—she looked to her brother—"was it six summers ago?"

"Aye, when it took half the city."

"But we're blessed, Bram and me," Elinor said. "We've stayed together and out of Bridewell."

"The gaol," Bram said, noticing Pen's puzzled look.

"And a dreadful place," Elinor said. "It's where they lock up women. Pickpockets, strumpets, and the like. And orphans, when the bailiffs can catch 'em."

"We've not been caught," Bram said.

"But how do you live?" Pen asked. "How do you pay the rent?"

Elinor glanced at Bram. "We don't actually pay rent," she said. "The house above is empty, so we've moved into the cellars."

"You must swear not to tell," Bram warned her.

"I'll not tell," Pen said. Then, thinking of Jory, she asked, "Do you steal for food?"

"We don't steal," Bram said gruffly.

"At first, we did," Elinor admitted. "Apples off a cart and whatnot. But we make an honest living now."

"Elinor plays her lute and sings," Bram said. "And I"—he bowed low with a flourish—"I play the fool, milady."

43

Elinor smiled. "Don't listen to him," she said. "He's a splendid juggler and magician."

Singer? Juggler? Magician? Pen was overwhelmed by such accomplishments. She never dreamed she would fall into such fine company in London.

"Me father acted on the stage," Pen said, then stopped. She had never spoken of Roger Banks and now felt shy discussing him with strangers. "But I never knew him," she added.

"No matter," Bram said cheerfully. "Performing's in the blood! You can join our band of players."

Pen stared at him. Did he mean it, or was he teasing her? "I . . . don't know how to juggle or play the lute," she said carefully.

"You can learn," Bram said. "Meantime, you know how to hold out a hat, don't you?"

Still wondering if he was serious, Pen said, "I can do that."

"I'd best see to supper," Elinor said. "Are you hungry, Pen?"

"Foolish question," Bram said, watching Pen's face. "Come. It's time you met the others."

7

ON PAINFUL LEGS, PEN followed them into a larger room, another cave buried in the earth. A lighted candle and the fire from the hearth warmed the crumbling walls. Four little boys sat around a table. When Pen came in, they stared, their eyes distrustful.

Elinor said, "You know Jory, of course. And there's Thomas, Ned, and Edom."

Pen wasn't certain which boy was which, for they all looked much the same, with their shabby clothes and hair in need of a trim. Only Jory's bright mop set him apart. None was older than nine or ten, and one was no more than six.

"Edom and me made two pennies blacking boots," an older boy said to Bram.

"Good lad, Thomas." Bram patted the boy on the back and ruffled another's hair.

"A gent give me a penny to watch his horse," the smallest boy piped up.

"Good for you, Ned," Bram said.

Jory, who was pouting, said nothing.

Elinor was stirring a pot over the fire. "I wonder where the others are," she said. "Well, there's no need to make the rest of you wait. They can eat when they get here." She began to fill bowls with stew.

Pen tried to eat slowly, but Elinor's mutton stew was the best meal she'd had in a long time. She cleaned her bowl before the boys were half-finished.

"There's more," Elinor said.

Pen was tempted, but who knew how many meals they would have to make from this one pot? She shook her head.

Elinor was clearing the table when Pen heard voices beyond a door that she assumed led to the street. The door opened, and a boy and girl ran in. The girl looked to be no older than six or seven, but she carried a heavy load in her drawn-up skirt.

"Look what we found!" The girl dropped her skirt and a flood of turnips and potatoes tumbled to the floor.

"Potatoes!" Jory cried. "Elinor, can we have potato soup?"

"Indeed we can," Elinor said. "Where did you get all this, Kitty?"

"The dustbin at the market," Kitty said happily. "They's hardly mushy or rotted at all." Then she noticed Pen and looked alarmed.

"This is Pen," Elinor said. "She'll be living with us now. Pen, meet Kitty and Walter."

Pen's eyes darted to Elinor. Then Bram hadn't been teasing about letting Pen stay? Elinor's smile reassured her. Pen's throat grew tight, and she looked away quickly.

When Kitty and Walter had joined the others at the table, Pen asked, "How do they all come to be here?"

"Thomas and Edom was neighbors," Bram said. "They lost their folks to the sickness the summer Da and Mam died, so they've always been with us. The others . . ." He shrugged. "They've just come along, one by one."

Elinor brought stew to the table for Kitty and Walter. They ate hungrily.

"Slowly," Elinor said. "Make it last."

Pen was glad she hadn't asked for more.

"Edom, pick up these potatoes and turnips," Bram said. "Jory can help you."

"Bring a sack," Edom said to Jory.

"I'm not your servant, now, am I?" Jory responded. "If you want a sack, you know where to find it."

Then Jory saw Bram's look. "All right," Jory muttered, and went to the cupboard for a sack.

When Kitty and Walter had eaten, Pen washed their bowls. She was stacking them in the cupboard when a girl wandered in from another room. A girl with a tangle of dark curls, wearing a black-and-crimson gown.

Pen turned and stared.

Rose yawned and stretched, obviously just waking up. She looked out of sorts and more rumpled than when Pen had last seen her.

"How can anyone sleep with all this yammering?" Rose demanded.

"Time you was up and out, anyhow," Jory said with a grin.

Rose scowled. "Shut your trap, you little sewer rat."

Jory just laughed.

When Rose saw Pen, she looked surprised, then amused. "Well, if it's not Mistress Mouse," she said. "How did you find your way here?"

"You might say a little sewer rat led me," Pen replied.

Jory laughed again, eyeing Pen with admiration.

Elinor looked puzzled. "You know each other?" she asked Rose.

But Rose seemed not to hear. She was staring hard at Pen. "It was Bram that found you, wasn't it? He brought me, too. Dragged me here kicking and screaming, he did."

Rose flashed Bram a smile. His face seemed to soften when he looked at her.

A curious stillness came over Elinor as she watched them. Then she turned away and filled a bowl with stew. She held it out to Rose.

Rose shook her head. "No time for supper."

A shadow passed over Elinor's face. "You needn't go, Rose. We've plenty of food to last the week."

"I'll pull me own weight," Rose said curtly. "I daresay I can take care of meself."

"Not this way," Elinor said.

Pen looked from one tense face to the other.

"Stay in tonight," Elinor said, a stubborn tone creeping into her voice.

"Leave me be," Rose said sharply. "What I do's no worse than begging for pennies."

Color flooded Elinor's face. "Will you speak to her, Bram?" she asked. "You're the only one she'll listen to."

Bram pulled Rose aside. The children went back to what they had been doing. Apparently, they had heard it all before. Elinor turned away and poured the bowl of stew back into the pot. But Pen didn't take her eyes off Bram and Rose. She couldn't hear what Bram was saying, but he looked troubled.

Rose listened for a moment, then began to shake her head. Bram frowned. His voice grew louder. "You don't have to live this way," Pen heard him say.

"I can live any way I please," Rose snapped.

"As you will, then," Bram said, and stalked away.

Rose put on her bonnet and tied the ribbons under her chin. She gave Bram a sassy smile and left without so much as a glance at the rest of them.

"You did all you could," Elinor said.

"Not enough," Bram said. He sounded tired.

Pen's curiosity was kindled. "Where did Rose go?" she asked. "Won't it be dark soon?"

The children snickered and gave Pen sly looks.

"That's when Rose does her work," Jory said. "In the dark."

The others laughed out loud and Elinor scolded them.

Bram saw Pen's bewilderment. "Men pay Rose to be with them," he said.

"She's a lady of the night," Jory said, looking at Pen as though she were a lackwit. "A strumpet!"

"Hush, Jory!" Elinor said.

Pen finally understood. Her cheeks grew warm with embarrassment. How ignorant she must seem. Why,

49

even the youngest here knew more than she did!

Bram was watching Pen. "Why did Rose call you 'Mistress Mouse'?" he asked.

"Because I come from the country, I suppose," Pen said, "and know so little about life in London."

"It's best *not* to know some things!" Elinor declared. Then to the children, she said, "It's off to bed with you."

"A song first," Ned said.

"Aye, sing to us," the others cried.

Elinor tried to look stern, but the children weren't fooled. They settled on the floor at her feet. Ned brought Elinor her lute.

She strummed the instrument and began to sing. Her voice was clear and strong, her eyes bright with devilment, as she sang a lively tune about a maid in search of her true love. The maid kissed every lad in the village, but none was just right.

> *So, it's time I was moving on, said she,*
> *Time I was moving on.*

The children laughed and sang with her. They leaped to their feet and began to dance. Pen was surprised when Jory pulled on her arm to dance with him. She had never learned to dance, but her feet seemed to know how to move with the music.

Before the evening was over, Pen had danced with Kitty and with all the little boys. Then Bram bowed and reached for her hand. They danced while the others watched and clapped—until Pen was breathless and

Bram fell to the floor laughing.

Pen lay awake after the others were asleep. Her eyelids were heavy, but she didn't want the day to end. She felt snug and safe in these cellars, surrounded by the comforting sounds of gentle snores and a child turning over in his sleep. She wanted the feelings to last.

For the first time since Mam was drowned, Pen didn't feel alone in the world. Because of Bram. And Elinor, and the children, too, of course. But it was Bram's kindness—and his laughter—that Pen thought about as she drifted toward sleep. And she found herself wondering if Bram was anything like her father when Roger Banks was young. When Mam had loved him, and he had brightened the earth with his presence.

8

ELINOR SERVED GRUEL AND thin slices of black bread for breakfast. The children chattered and squabbled while they gulped down their food. To Pen, who had known only the quiet voice of her mother all her life, the children seemed rowdy. But they were so like a family as they teased and bickered among themselves that Pen was drawn to them.

"You can come with Elinor and me today," Bram said to Pen.

"As can Master Jory," Elinor added. "To keep you out of trouble," she said to the boy.

Jory watched unhappily as the others left to search for work. "I know where there's wood we can use for kindling," he said hopefully. "I can show Thomas and Edom."

"You can tell 'em just as well," Bram said.

Jory sighed.

"Come on," Bram said to the boy. "We're losing money standing here."

Pen and Jory followed Bram and Elinor out the door

and up a flight of uneven stairs. Bram opened the door to the street and looked outside.

"All clear," he said.

Houses with sagging roofs and rotting timbers squatted on either side of the muddy street. Men slouched on doorsteps, smoking their pipes. Women in ragged gowns poured slop into the street and shouted at dirty children.

Elinor and Bram walked briskly, avoiding the eyes of their neighbors. They turned onto one street after another, until Pen was hopelessly lost. Finally, they made their way down a street of grand houses to an open area. A park, Bram called it.

Ladies in beautiful gowns and bonnets strolled the brick paths, holding the hands of quiet children. Men wearing fine coats and hats sat on benches under the trees.

Elinor sat down on a low wall. Bram handed his battered cap to Pen.

"When a crowd gathers," he said, "just walk through with me cap held out."

Elinor began to strum the lute and sing. A few people stopped to listen. Bram dug into a sack and brought out apples. He tossed an apple into the air, then another, and another, until he was juggling four. Ladies smiled and children clapped their hands.

More people gathered. Pen watched as Bram kept the apples circling in the air. He strolled the path, tossing the apples behind his back and spinning around to catch them. This feat delighted the crowd. They laughed and applauded. A few reached into their pockets and purses.

Bram's cap began to fill with coins.

Pen witnessed many of Bram's tricks that day. She saw him reach behind a child's ear and bring forth a penny. She watched him cover his empty hand with a cloth and whisk it away to reveal a turnip. She clapped with all the rest as he walked on his hands, danced to Elinor's music, and turned somersaults in midair.

When the crowd grew bored and drifted away, Elinor and Bram moved to another location. Before the day was over, Pen was sure she had seen every park and square in London.

Jory had been told to stay with Elinor, but Pen sometimes noticed him moving into the crowd. She wondered whose purse he was snatching. Then Bram would catch the boy's eye and Jory would come back reluctantly.

Pen was fascinated by Elinor's and Bram's skill, and elated when their audience rewarded them with coins. But Pen wondered what Mam would think of her acting the beggar. Mam, who was too proud to bow her head to anyone.

The sun was low in the sky when the four made their way toward home. They were tired and hungry, but Pen felt happy. It had been a good money day. Bram had said there were enough pennies in his pocket to buy bread and ale for the week, and a bit of stew meat, besides. But as they approached their house, Pen saw a man beating a cart horse, until she wondered how the wretched creature was left standing. Despite its beautiful parks and houses, Pen didn't like this city as much as she had thought she would.

The other children were waiting in the cellar, but they were strangely quiet. Elinor noticed at once. "What's wrong?" she asked. "Your silence causes me to fear the worst."

Rose was sitting at the table with a mug of ale. "The bailiff saw Thomas and Edom making off with a bit of wood," she said. "Chased 'em and near caught 'em, he did."

Alarm showed in Elinor's face. "Did he see you come here?"

"Nay," Thomas said. "We led him on a merry chase, we did. Run him down to the river and lost him on the quay."

Elinor still looked anxious. "We'll stay inside a few days," she said. "In case the bailiff's watching for you."

"Do as you will," Rose said, "but I'm on me way out."

"You'll stay in tonight," Bram said firmly. "We don't want you carted off to Bridewell."

"And haven't I been there before?" she demanded. "There's nothing at Bridewell I can't handle."

"You're not the only one living here!" Elinor reminded her. "Have you forgotten the children? I'd not care to see 'em hauled off to the gaol with you."

Rose's eyes narrowed. They shifted from Elinor to Pen. "Aye, there's some that wouldn't stand a chance in Bridewell," she said.

"Can it be so bad?" Pen bristled. "You look none the worse for it."

"Are rats the size of tomcats so bad?" Rose shot back. "And women kept in darkness 'til they've gone stark mad? They'll claw your eyes out," Rose said with quiet satisfaction, "and gulp 'em down for supper."

"That's enough!" Elinor cried.

"No one goes outside 'til I say they can," Bram said.

Even so, Pen was surprised when night came and Rose settled down with another mug of ale, making no move to leave the cellar. Pen watched while Bram taught the children magic tricks. She could feel Rose's keen eyes on her from time to time, and she wondered what she'd done to earn the girl's contempt.

After the children were bedded down, Pen helped Elinor clean up. Then she brought Bram a mug of ale and sat at the table with him.

"Why do the bailiffs waste their time with children," she asked, "when there are thieves and murderers in the streets?"

"It's the king's order to lock up orphans," Bram said. "He considers them filthy and loathsome, an affront to the eye, and a nuisance with their begging."

"Mayhap we should leave London," Elinor said.

"And go where?" Bram asked.

Rose watched them over the edge of her mug and said nothing.

9

AFTER THREE DAYS INSIDE, the children's pent-up energy bubbled over into constant fussing and fighting. Rose was arguing with everyone, especially Elinor, and even Bram had grown short-tempered. Pen didn't think she could bear captivity another day.

Rose must have reached the same conclusion, for that evening she appeared wearing her bonnet and started for the door.

"Where do you think you're going?" Elinor demanded crossly.

"Better a fortnight in Bridewell than locked up here another minute," Rose said.

"Bram hasn't said you can go."

"Consider it said," Bram said gruffly. "I've grown weary of being everyone's gaoler."

Elinor looked startled. "But the bailiff—"

"Hang the bailiff!" Bram exclaimed. "We can't stay buried like corpses forever."

Rose ran to Bram and kissed him on the cheek. The

children giggled and elbowed one another. Elinor's face froze.

Rose danced out the door, looking like an excited child on her way to a party. Pen watched her go, all the while wondering why she was feeling so cross herself. It was none of her concern that Rose kissed Bram, nor that he seemed to like it.

While Pen cleaned up after supper, she found herself wondering about Rose—where the girl had come from, and how she came to live on London's streets.

"How long has Rose been with you?" Pen asked Elinor.

"Forever, it seems," Elinor said brusquely. "But I suppose it's been no more than two years."

"She's an orphan, then?"

"Apparently," Bram said. "Not that she's said much. Rose isn't one to bare her soul. She did say her mother died when she was small. After that, an aunt took her in, then some other relations. I'm under the impression they treated her ill—beat her, I'll wager. She ran away when she was twelve, and she's lived by her wits ever since."

"We don't know about a father," Elinor said.

"I doubt that Rose does, either," Bram said. "Her mother made a living on the streets. She may not have known herself who Rose's father was."

With these few words, Pen's judgment of Rose became less harsh. No matter that Rose was prone to be sharp-tongued and selfish. Pen could look past that now—to the motherless child left to fend for herself.

* * *

Life returned to normal in the cellars—or as normal as living underground and sneaking in and out like a criminal could ever be. Sometimes at night, as she lay on her pile of sacks, listening to the others' snores and sighs, Pen remembered her quiet life with Mam. She thought about watching the moon rise through the cottage window and resting her face against the goats' warm sides as she milked them. She would never miss the village, nor the villagers. But she did miss the sight of the ever-changing moon, the whisper of tall grass blowing in the wind, the serenade of a throstle. And most of all, she missed Mam. Sometimes Pen still woke in the mornings expecting to see Mam's smile and to hear her say, "Fair morn, Mistress Lazybones."

As Pen became accustomed to walking through the crowds with Bram's cap, she added some touches of her own. She learned to smile sweetly at the ladies, looking young and innocent. She lifted sad eyes to gentlemen who were ready to hurry away, prompting them to pause just long enough to dig into their pockets and produce a penny for the cap. When Bram saw they were taking home more coins, he showered Pen with praise. Pen delighted in his approval, but she wasn't comfortable with her role of street beggar. She decided it was time to find work of her own.

That evening, Pen said to Bram, "If I had a hook and line, I could catch fish to sell and bring in some money of me own."

Seeing a way to escape his long, tedious days with Bram and Elinor, Jory said, "I could help her! With baiting the hook and carrying the fish to market."

"It might not be a bad idea," Bram said thoughtfully. "But Pen, you're making us rich with those doe eyes of yours."

"Kitty could pass the hat," Pen said. "She's so tiny and pretty, she'd spur 'em to dig deep."

"Please, Bram!" Kitty exclaimed. "I can do it!"

Bram looked from one hopeful face to the other. "It seems to have been decided," he said.

After supper, Elinor played the lute and sang.

> *I am a wandering troubadour*
> *And I shall sing for you*
> *The ballad of a maid most fair,*
> *Her grace and charm beyond compare,*
> *Her heart forever true.*
>
> *I am a wandering troubadour*
> *And I shall sing for you*
> *A madrigal of my own sweet love,*
> *Her eyes as clear as the stars above,*
> *And her heart forever true.*

The children stirred restlessly and began to fidget. They were bored by the slow-moving song. Pen watched Bram, who was stretched out on a bench with his eyes closed. For the first time, she noticed the few pale freckles across his nose, the fine curls as soft as a child's along his hairline, the full curve of his lower lip.

Pen was startled by the wave of tenderness that

60

swept over her. She turned away, feeling baffled.

Elinor finished the song and sent the children to bed. Pen left the room without looking at Bram. When he called out good night, the children responded, but Pen lay silent on her pallet. Her heart was brimming, so full of sweetness and wonder, she thought it might burst. She hadn't known that happiness could be so painful.

She was still staring into the darkness much later when she heard a noise.

Pen sat straight up and listened. She heard the noise again. It was a door opening. Then she heard footsteps, slow and measured, as they made their way across the floor overhead.

Pen shot up off her pallet and felt her way through the darkness to the main room. "Bram," she whispered. "Are you awake? Did you hear—"

"We heard," Bram said softly.

"They've found us." This was Elinor's frightened voice. "The children—"

"Hush," Bram said.

Pen made her way to the corner where Bram and Elinor crouched.

The tread of boots on the floorboards above grew louder. They were moving toward the staircase that led to the cellars.

Bram's arm slipped around Pen's shoulder. She buried her face in his chest and clenched her eyes shut. Her heart pounded against her ribs.

Another door opened. Boots thumped down the stairs. Pen's instinct told her to run. But where? The staircase was the only way out of the cellars.

Bram pushed Pen to the floor. Lying prone on the damp earth, Pen scarcely dared breathe for fear that she would be heard.

The footsteps moved closer. Then, just as one of the children cried out in his sleep, the door burst open.

Torchlight flooded the room. Men swarmed in, knocking over benches, sending crockery crashing to the floor.

Pen leaped up, but one of the men grabbed her before she could run. Bram struck her captor in the face. Another man hit Bram on the head with a cudgel. Bram slumped to the floor and didn't move.

Elinor cried out and crawled toward Bram. She was grabbed before she could reach him.

Pen struggled to free herself, but her hands were being tied and a rope was slipped around her neck. Over her assailant's shoulder, she could see Kitty and the little boys standing wide-eyed and terrified in the doorway. Ned was crying.

"Round 'em all up," one of the men said.

"A pox on you!" Pen screamed at the man who held her. She kicked him in the shin.

He cried out and jerked the rope around her neck. She gasped for air.

"This un's a little wildcat," the man said. He drew Pen around to face him and grinned. How hideous he was! With a tangle of greasy hair and a scraggle of beard and puckered scars around an eye that drooped and gazed blindly at Pen. He brought his loathsome face close to hers, and he spat.

The wetness ran down Pen's cheek and neck.

"Bram!" she cried.

But Bram lay unmoving on the floor, his face covered with blood.

One of the men dragged Elinor toward the door. The others were tying up Kitty and the boys. Fighting against the ropes, Jory bit down hard on one of the men's hands.

The man yelped. "Lice-ridden little cur!" he screeched. Then he hit the boy over the head and Jory slid limply to the floor.

The men pushed and dragged them through the door and up the stairs. Pen still struggled to free herself, but the ropes were too strong.

"They's a sorry lot," one of the men said as he pushed Elinor and Kitty up the steps.

"But worth a pretty penny," another responded.

The man behind Pen said, "Jamestown's the place for this 'un," and gave her a shove.

Pen tripped on the stairs. Her captor laughed.

"And wouldn't I like to be there when they teach her some manners," he said. "Seven years they'll work you in Virginia, lass." He yanked her head up and said softly into her ear, "Seven long years in hell."

10

PEN LAY VERY STILL in a pile of foul-smelling straw. She was afraid to move, lest others crammed into the dark space take notice and do her harm. There were no windows in the room, and only the one door of thick iron bars. A single torch outside the cell did little to warm the stone walls and floor.

Elinor had finally drifted off to sleep. Kitty was curled against Elinor's back, whimpering as she dreamed. Around them, women muttered and cursed, cried and shouted obscenities. Sometimes, for no apparent reason, one of the women would fly at another, pulling at her hair and clawing her face. But most of the women slumped listlessly against the walls like piles of discarded rags. They made no attempt to move, not even to relieve themselves, and wallowed in their own waste.

Pen felt as though she had been delivered into the pit of hell, and there was no one to know or care. Mam would have cared, but Mam was gone. Pen turned on her side and squeezed her eyes shut. Even so, she felt the sting of tears and had to blink them away.

Elinor groaned in her sleep, then jerked awake, her eyes wild with terror. Pen reached for her hand, but Elinor wrenched away and drew herself up into a ball. Awakened by the movement, Kitty began to cry.

"Elinor, it's me, Pen." She shook Elinor gently. "You're frightening Kitty."

Elinor's eyes darted to Pen, then to the little girl who lay sobbing beside her. A deep sigh escaped Elinor's lips.

"God's blood," Elinor whispered, and stroked Kitty's hair. "What's to become of us?"

Pen sat up slowly and leaned against the cold wall. Her wrists and throat burned where the rope had cut into her flesh. Her legs and arms ached from fighting to free herself. But her thoughts had turned to Bram and the boys. She feared for Bram and Jory, especially, with the hard blows they had taken from their captors. The last time she saw them, they were being carried up the stairs, as lifeless as heaps of bones.

Kitty had stopped crying. She snuggled into Elinor's lap and fell into an exhausted sleep.

Pen surveyed the shadowy figures around her. Gathering up her courage, she asked, "Do any of you know what they do with the men and boys?"

"Locks 'em up the same as us," a woman answered. "Though I doubt they have such lovely accommodations."

Some of the women laughed, but there was no warmth in the sound.

A woman with limp yellow hair peered into Pen's face. "Caught by the spirits, was you?"

"It could've been the bailiff's men," Elinor said.

"Nay, it weren't the hawks that swooped down on you," the woman said. She was no more than skin over bones, and most of her teeth were gone.

"What are spirits?" Pen asked Elinor.

"Never mind," Elinor muttered.

"Spirits?" The yellow-haired woman grinned at Pen. "They roams the streets in search of lads and lasses, and spirits 'em away. Well paid for their trouble, they is."

"Hush up, woman," Elinor said crossly.

"Name's Mary," the woman said. "I don't think I've had the pleasure."

"Nor will you," Elinor snapped.

Pen looked at Elinor, perplexed by her rudeness, then back at Mary. "Why do the spirits catch children?"

"They's shipped to Jamestown, that's what," Mary said with a sly glance at Elinor. "For cert you've heard about Jamestown, lass. In Virginia? The underside of hell, that's what I hear. If hard usage and starvation don't kill you, then the savages will."

"Where is this Virginia?"

"Pen, will you cease with your questions?" Elinor demanded. "Virginia's nothing to do with you."

"Sad to say, but it is!" an old woman responded. She was hunched against the wall next to Pen. "Virginia's across the sea," she said to Pen. "And a vile place it is, though it be the king's colony. Few that goes there lives past a season, and they's always needing more to work the fields."

"That's why the spirits brung you here," Mary said. She turned to the old woman. "Tell her, Jane."

Jane nodded. "Aye, it's God's own truth, lass. They'll keep you here 'til there's a ship sailing for Virginia. If you survive the sea passage, they'll sell you to a planter to slave in his fields."

"This hole's a paradise next to Virginia," Mary said. "I'm happy not to go meself."

"It's death awaits you either way, eh?" Jane said.

"Shut your mouth, crone!" Mary shouted. "You've not seen me sentence carried out."

"Not yet," Jane said.

Pen felt a sudden chill. Her eyes darted to Mary. "What are you here for?" she asked.

Mary made a garbled sound and turned away.

"She killed her husband," Jane said cheerfully. "Took an ax and chopped him into so many bits, they never did find 'em all!"

"I never!" Mary screamed, looking as though she meant to leap on the old woman and gouge her eyes out. "I never took the ax to him. Never!" Tears spilled from her eyes and trailed down her hollow cheeks.

"Then it was the little people, most likely," Jane said placidly.

Their one meal a day was a piece of bread and a little water. The water was brackish, with a strong smell to it. Pen gulped it down anyway, for her throat and lips felt parched. She feared she was getting the fever that plagued so many of the women, but she kept this worry to herself. Elinor was still distraught and didn't need more to add to her burden.

Kitty had finished her bread and leaned listlessly against Elinor's shoulder. "I'm still hungry," she said.

Elinor broke her remaining bread in two and gave the larger piece to Kitty. Seeing this, Pen felt ashamed, for she'd gobbled down her own portion without a thought for anyone else.

She was no longer certain how long they'd been there. At first, she kept count of the days by how often they were fed, but the days had become too many. In any case, she was certain that spring had passed, and mayhap summer, as well.

Nearby, a woman called Anna sat in the straw, holding a rag in the crook of her arm as though it were a baby. For lack of anything better to do, Pen watched Anna rock the piece of cloth and murmur to it. Her son had been born in this terrible place, but he hadn't lived to draw a dozen breaths. Anna refused to believe her child was dead and fought the gaolers when they came to carry the little body away. It had taken three men to hold her down and wrench the infant from her arms.

"How can you stand to watch her day after day?" Elinor asked softly.

Pen shrugged. "If I look away, there's only something else to break the heart."

Elinor sighed and said nothing. She couldn't argue with the truth of this. There was Anna, gone stark mad. And Mary waiting for her hanging. And others writhing with fever and no one to tend them. Sometimes Elinor gave her own allotment of water to one with fever, but more often than not, the woman just spewed it up and died anyway.

"That babe was the lucky one," Pen said, her eyes still resting on Anna. "He was able to leave this torment."

"Aye," Elinor said, and lay down with Kitty to try to sleep.

11

"PEN, WAKE UP!"

She opened her eyes and saw Elinor leaning over her. "What?" Pen mumbled.

"It's Kitty," Elinor said.

There was something in Elinor's voice that brought Pen instantly awake. She crawled over to where Kitty lay. The girl's eyes were closed and she didn't move. Pen pressed her ear to Kitty's chest and heard nothing. No beat of the heart, no intake of breath. She reached for Kitty's hand and it was cold—like Mam's the last time Pen had touched it.

Pen sat back on her heels. "She's gone."

"Nay!" Elinor shook her head furiously. "She only took the fever two days ago."

"She was too weak to fight it," Pen said.

Elinor pulled Kitty into her arms and wept softly.

Pen crawled back to her space against the wall. She hadn't taken the fever after all, but she wished she had instead of Kitty. Pen's eyes came to rest on the child in Elinor's arms. She looked away quickly, unable to bear seeing Kitty so pale and still. Not while in her mind Pen could still picture the little girl running into the cellars, flushed and windblown, and so proud of a skirtful of spoiled potatoes and turnips.

Pen turned her face to the wall. She heard the rustle of straw, and then Elinor was beside her. Elinor was wiping away tears, but her eyes only filled again.

Nay, Pen thought, don't do this. She didn't think she could shoulder Elinor's grief along with her own.

"What do you suppose they'll do with her?" Elinor asked, her voice thick with tears.

"I don't know," Pen said softly.

"They'll give her a proper burial, though," Elinor said anxiously. Then, her voice rising like a wail, she said, "Oh, Pen, how could all this have happened to us?"

Pen just shook her head. Then she reached out to Elinor, and, holding on to each other, they cried.

Late that night, Pen woke up feeling stiff and cold. Beside her, Elinor was murmuring a prayer. What good does praying do? Pen wondered. Would it help them get out of here? Pen had little hope of ever being free again, but she would rather die than stay in this dark hole forever. Even transport to the dreadful place called Virginia seemed better than this.

Pen's smile was bitter when it occurred to her that her last hope lay in being exiled to a land where she would most surely die.

A few days later, they came for Mary. All her bluster crumbled when the men pulled her to her feet and chained her hands together.

"It's a mistake!" she cried. "I did nothing! Nothing!"

Except for Mary's voice, the room was silent. For the first time since Pen and Elinor had been brought there, no one screeched or cursed or wailed. Elinor gripped Pen's hand so tightly, her nails cut into Pen's flesh.

Mary began to weep as they led her toward the door. "Have pity," she pleaded though her sobs. "I pray you, take pity on me!" Her head jerked as she searched in panic for someone to help her.

"Jane?" Mary cried, but the old woman stared at the floor and refused to look up.

Then Mary's terrified eyes fell on Pen.

A shiver ran through Pen and she began to tremble. *Nay,* Pen groaned inwardly, *I can do nothing!* She longed to turn away, but the horror in those eyes held her.

Mary was breathing hard, her nostrils flaring, then closing, like the gills of a fish. She lifted her chained hands toward Pen in a desperate plea, and one of the gaolers slapped them down. The flash of anguish in Mary's face was more than Pen could bear. She ran to the woman and clasped Mary's shaking hands between her own. The gaolers appeared startled. Then they seemed to realize that this scrap of a girl posed no danger. They looked away, as if embarrassed by the scene.

"Have mercy on me," Mary whispered.

"God will have mercy on you," Pen said.

Mary's head snapped up. Her eyes seemed unfocused as they sought out Pen's face. "Will He?" she asked, tears still flowing. "No matter what . . . I've done?"

"No matter what you've done," Pen said softly.

Mary sighed, and Pen felt the woman's body go limp. The gaolers led Mary, stumbling, to the door. She didn't resist.

"God keep you," Pen said to her retreating back. But Mary gave no sign that she had heard.

The heavy door clanged shut behind her. Pen stood at the bars, watching until Mary was out of sight. It was Pen who wept now, her heart spilling over with pity for the woman. Elinor came to stand with her. And all around them was silence.

Pen awoke the next morning to shrieks and laughter. A few of the women were pressed against the bars of the door, calling out to someone they knew.

"Move away!" the gaoler shouted as he unlocked the door. He shoved someone inside and slammed the door shut again.

"So you're back!" one of the women cried. "Missing home, was you?"

"I was longing for the sight of your ugly face, I was," came the cheerful reply.

Pen knew that voice. She shot up off the floor and brushed the hair from her eyes.

A figure swished toward her and said, "Well, if it's not Mistress Mouse."

"Rose? "

"In the flesh," Rose said.

Pen looked from the tangled curls to the black-and-crimson gown—now more ripped and stained than ever—and back to the red lips that were curved into a sassy smile. Inexplicably, Pen's eyes filled with tears.

"Now, don't go welling up on me," Rose said. "You'll get me gown all soggy."

Elinor was watching them. "So the spirits caught you, too," she said without emotion.

"Spirits? Nay!" Rose exclaimed. "A pesky hawk tried to run me off me turf, that's what. So me knuckles did some damage to his jaw."

"You slugged a hawk?" The women laughed with delight. "If you're not too much, you darling girl!"

Elinor's eyes hadn't moved from Rose's face. "You must have known," she said slowly, "that they'd haul you off to the gaol for striking a bailiff."

"Not for long," Rose said. "As I've heard, we'll be sailing any day for the New World."

A startling realization came to Pen. "You had yourself thrown in here on purpose," she said, "to be with us when we're shipped to Virginia."

"Don't be daft!" Rose said. "Why would I give up me easy life to go with you? If you must know, it was Elinor's stew I was missing."

"And a fine meal they'll serve you here," Elinor said. A glimmer of life had come back to her eyes.

"Me thought exactly!" Rose said in her brash way. "Now, where's me bed? Pile up some straw, Mouse. Nice and thick, mind you. I've had a tiring day."

Later, as they sat together eating their bread, Rose asked, "Where's Kitty?"

"The fever took her," Elinor said.

Rose looked stunned. Then her face twisted into a scowl and she bit fiercely into her bread.

"If they send us to Virginia, we'll see Bram," Pen said. "And the boys."

"If they're still alive," Elinor said harshly. She glanced at Rose. "You're a fool to give up your freedom. You know that, don't you?"

Rose opened her mouth to speak, then stopped, frowning at Pen. "What do you think you're grinning at, Mouse?"

Pen shrugged, still smiling. "It's just good to have you here," she said.

Rose grunted and surveyed the dismal room. "Ain't it just a palace, though?" she said.

September 1627
The Atlantic

12

LIGHTED BY ONLY ONE oil lantern, the ship's underdeck was as dark as the cells at Bridewell, and even more cramped. At least a hundred people were being herded into the close space, the men and boys chained together in pairs.

Pen followed Elinor and Rose through the snarl of bodies. A seaman prodded them along with a truncheon. Pen stepped over a pair of long, outstretched legs and peered down into the owner's face to see if they belonged to Bram. She sighed when she saw that the man was old, with a head as smooth as a newborn babe's.

"Move on, move on," the seaman shouted over the drone of voices. "Wenches to the rear."

Elinor looked at Pen over her shoulder. "Have you seen 'em?" she asked.

"Not yet."

"Hurry up," the sailor barked.

Pen stepped around one body, only to collide with another.

"Watch it!" came a boy's sharp cry. "Clumsy oaf," he muttered.

Pen couldn't make out the face in the dim light, but she knew the voice. "Jory?"

"Aye," the boy said warily. "And who's asking?"

"Jory, it's Pen!" In her excitement, she forgot the sailor pressing her to move along, and she stooped to hug Jory. "Are you well? Are the other boys here? Where's Bram?"

"Bram's around," Jory said. "And Thomas and Edom. Gaol fever took Walter and Ned."

How many more will be lost? Pen thought. She squeezed the boy's hand. But before she could speak, the seaman yanked her up and pushed her after the other women.

"I saw Jory," Pen said as she was shoved into a dark corner with Elinor and Rose.

"And Bram?" Rose asked.

"Nay, but he's here," Pen said. "Walter and Ned didn't make it," she added softly.

Tears sprang to Elinor's eyes, but they didn't fall. Her face turned hard.

They sat down among the other women and were silent. There was just enough room to stretch out on the plank floor.

Finally, Elinor said, "We could shout Bram's name."

"He'd never hear us over all the noise," Rose said.

"We can look for him later," Pen said, "once the beady-eyes with their sticks are gone."

"Who says they'll go?" Elinor asked.

"I daresay they'll find a spot with more breeze to make the voyage," Pen said.

She wiped her damp face on her sleeve and wrinkled her nose. The heat was stifling, but even worse was the stink of vomit and foul waste. It seemed to rise from the floorboards like steam off hot stones after a rain.

"Not even a bit of straw to lie on?" one of the women complained.

"It's spoiled, you are," another replied, "by the comforts of Bridewell."

Some of the women snickered. Pen lay down on the rough planks and turned her back to them. She didn't feel like hearing their foolish talk.

"Here, poppet," a voice said into her ear. "Rest your head on this."

Pen looked over her shoulder and saw a little woman with white hair kneeling beside her. The woman was holding out a bundle of rags.

Pen was caught off guard by the stranger's kindness. "You keep it," she said. The words came out sounding ungrateful. "You'll need it before we see land again," she added.

"I don't expect to make the full journey," the woman said calmly. "I'm old, you see."

Pen sat up and looked into the woman's face. It was crisscrossed with wrinkles, the skin gathered in loose pouches beneath her dark eyes. But the eyes were sharp. They wouldn't miss much, Pen thought.

"I'm Grace Simon," the woman said.

"Pen Downing."

"You're a pretty little thing," Grace said. "Me youngest daughter looked a bit like you when she was a girl."

"Is she here with you?"

The woman shook her head slightly. "Nay," she said. "It's only me."

The sailors left to go above deck. They locked the hatch door behind them.

"We can look for Bram now," Pen said to Elinor and Rose.

"Would Bram be your brother?" Grace asked.

"*Her* brother," Pen said, nodding toward Elinor.

"And your sweetheart?" Grace persisted.

"Nay," Pen said quickly.

There were more men than women belowdecks, and Pen stared into many faces before she recognized one. It was Edom she found first, who pointed across a man's round belly to Thomas. The boys were glad to see Pen and Rose, but it was Elinor they fell on like babes returned to their mother.

"Have you kept well?" Elinor fretted, touching their cheeks with the back of her hand. "No fever, but you're all bones. Would that I could fatten you up with some of me stew."

"You can fatten us when we get to Virginia," Edom said.

"Is it certain that's where we're bound?" Pen asked.

"The crew said so when we came on board."

"They need us for the tobacco," came a voice from behind them.

Pen spun around. Aye, it was Bram standing there. But he was changed. The youthful fullness of his face had given way to sunken cheeks and weary eyes. A reddish scar puckered the skin at his temple.

Without thinking, Pen reached out to touch the scar. Bram jerked his head away. "It's healed," he said. "But not so pretty, eh?"

His voice had changed as much as his appearance. It had grown bitter.

"Bram!" Elinor flung her arms around him and began to cry.

Rose held back, watching—appearing almost shy, Pen thought. Then, not realizing that she was being observed, Rose gazed into Bram's face with a look of such grave tenderness that Pen was stunned. Rose had hidden her feelings behind sassy words and brazen kisses; only now, Pen saw the truth: Rose was in love with Bram. But surely Bram couldn't feel anything in return, Pen thought hastily. He wanted better for Rose—he might like her, even pity her—but he certainly didn't love her! Pen refused to consider that the discomfort she was feeling might be jealousy.

"What have you heard about Jamestown?" Elinor was asking Bram.

Rose seemed to snap back to the present. She dropped her eyes. Pen roused herself from the shock she felt and turned her attention to Bram.

"Rich men in England are backing the colony," he said. "Friends of the king. They trust they'll grow richer on the tobacco raised in Virginia. That's why they need indentured servants—to work the tobacco fields."

"But what good are children to them?" Elinor asked. She looked down at Edom leaning against her.

"Children don't eat much," Bram said, "and when they drop in their tracks, there's always a ship bringing more."

"Can Jamestown be any worse than Bridewell?" Pen asked. "At least we'll see daylight and breathe fresh air."

"Better to have died in the gaol than be owned by another man," Bram said. The bitterness had crept back into his voice.

They felt the ship move. Its timbers creaked and groaned as the vessel crawled away from the quay. Women fell to their knees and sobbed in despair for loved ones left behind, and for a homeland they might never see again.

An old man rose to his feet and began to pray. The others grew silent to listen.

Lord, may we know Thy mercy in our hour of need. And if it be Thy will that our earthly lives should end on this voyage, let it be swift, dear Lord. Let it be swift.

13

WHEN THEY WERE TWO days out to sea, the men and boys
were released from their chains.

"But if you try coming above deck, you'll be the worse
for it," one of the seamen warned them.

Now Bram and the boys could move about freely, or
as freely as was possible in the crowded space. They sat
with Pen, Elinor, and Rose to eat their breakfast. Elinor
took a bite of her hard biscuit, then gave it to Jory.

Bram studied her pale face. "Are you not well?" he
asked.

"It's this pitching and rolling," Elinor said. "I can't
keep food down."

Pen was feeling queasy herself from the rocking of
the ship. She listened to the wind howling overhead and
wondered if the vessel was sturdy enough to withstand a
gale.

As day passed into evening, the wind picked up.
When the crewmen opened the hatch to bring down supper, rain poured into the underdeck. Some of the passengers were too ill to care about food, but others swarmed

around the men, grabbing for pieces of salt pork and dark bread.

"There's worms in this meat," a woman grumbled.

"They'll be gone soon enough," Rose said, biting into the pork with relish.

Bram laughed and winked at Rose. A bit of the old Bram, Pen thought. She was happy to see his high spirits restored, but the smug look on Rose's face rankled. As if she were the only one who could coax a smile from Bram.

Elinor still couldn't eat. She curled up in a corner and turned her back to them. When she began to retch, it was the old woman Grace who held Elinor's head and wiped her face.

After supper, Pen went to sit with Elinor. Thankfully, Elinor was finally asleep.

"Poor lassie," Grace murmured, stroking Elinor's curls. They were matted with filth from the gaol, but Grace didn't seem to care.

"How many children have you?" Pen asked.

"Six," Grace said, her face lighting up at the thought of them. "Four boys and two girls. And fourteen grand-children."

Pen wondered what the old woman was doing on this wretched ship, away from her family.

"It was me husband sent me here," Grace said, as though reading Pen's thoughts. "I was pretty once," she said, her voice wistful, "but I'm old and ugly now. He grew tired of me."

"You mean he brought you to the ship against your will?"

"Paid others to do it," Grace said. "Me husband's an innkeeper. One night, two men grabbed me outside the inn. Threw a sack over me head and bound me. But I heard him when he was paying 'em. It was me William, all right. And don't I know his voice after thirty years?"

"What a wicked thing to do!" Pen exclaimed.

"Aye, it was that," Grace said. Then suddenly, her eyes sparkled with devilment. "I only hope he's having a high time now," she remarked, "for what he paid to be done with me."

The seas quieted overnight. By morning, sunlight showed around the hatch door. Elinor sat up and ate a little.

After breakfast, a sailor opened the hatch. Women and small children could go above deck, he said, but men and older boys must stay below.

"They need fresh air and a leg stretch same as us," Rose protested.

"I see how *you'd* be thinking of the men," the crewman said, leering at her fancy dress, which now hung in tatters. "But you'll have to ply your trade belowdecks!"

Rose's eyes flashed and Pen thought the girl might fly into him. But Elinor grabbed Rose's arm and pushed her toward the hatch. "Don't listen to him," she said. "I need your help."

The sunlight was so bright after the darkness belowdecks, it hurt Pen's eyes. But the breeze felt good against her skin and cleared away the nasty smells from below. She went to the rail and leaned over to receive the cool sea spray in her face. When her hair was soaked, she wrung it out and combed her fingers through it. She took the wet hem of her dress and scrubbed at the grime on her hands and arms. But when she noticed the sailors peering at her bare legs, she dropped her skirt and glared at them.

"Help us, Pen," Elinor said.

Rose and Elinor were holding their petticoats and the boys' shirts into the spray. Pen picked up two ragged shirts at Elinor's feet and dangled them over the rail. The taste on her lips was salty, and the spray burned her tongue. But what a glorious feeling to stand in the wind and be showered with cold, clean water.

Pen felt almost happy as she and the others were herded below. How long had it been since she'd felt the wind and sun on her face? How could she have ever taken such joys for granted?

Elinor lay down to rest. Pen helped Rose drape the shirts and petticoats over barrels to dry.

"They smell of fish," Jory said, wrinkling his nose.

"And sunshine," Pen said.

Bram pulled Pen aside. "Elinor worries me," he said. "The others are over their pukish stomachs, but she's still weak."

"She needs food and rest, that's all," Pen assured him.

"We'll make her strong again," Bram said. "We must

all be strong when we reach Virginia, and ready to escape at the first chance."

"Escape? But how? As I hear it," Pen said, "Virginia's nothing but wilderness. Where would we go?"

"I met a sailor in the gaol who's been to Virginia," Bram whispered so that no one else could hear. "It's as bad as we've been told. But he said others have escaped from Jamestown to colonies in the north. They worked their way back to England aboard a ship."

"You might be able to crew on a ship," Pen said. "But what of Elinor and Rose and me?"

"If you cut your hair and donned men's breeches," Bram said, "you'd look no less a man than the blighters crewing this rust bucket."

Then he smiled. It was very nearly the old crooked grin that had first charmed Pen—though not quite. Even so, for the first time since the spirits had dragged them off to the gaol, she felt a shred of hope.

14

ON SATURDAY NIGHTS, the crew brought them as much gin as they could drink.

"It's not for our pleasure," Bram said. "We're easier to handle half-drunk."

It was true that many of the men, and some of the women and children as well, drank themselves into a stupor and weren't heard from again until the following day. Their silence was a blessing. But some spent the night vomiting gin all over the rest of them.

Grace amazed the others by how much drink she could hold. "I spent me life serving spirits and taking a nip along," Grace said. "Only the ones I served was watered," she added with a twinkle. "Them I drunk me-self was pure."

Gradually, the air turned cooler, then cold. At night, Pen snuggled against Elinor and Rose for warmth. "Like a litter of kittens," Rose said. When they washed their clothing over the side of the ship, their fingers were soon numb.

Pen and Bram watched Elinor with growing concern.

She only picked at her food and seemed to be wasting away. One morning, she didn't get up for breakfast.

"Elinor, you must eat," Pen said, holding out a biscuit to her.

"They try to poison us with their putrid food," Elinor said weakly.

"Aye, but we've not keeled over yet," Rose said. "Take just a bite," she coaxed.

Bram looked anxiously into his sister's face. "You must try, love," he said.

Elinor was shivering. "It's so cold," she murmured. "Can I have another blanket, Mam?"

Bram and Pen exchanged a look.

"She's out of her head," Rose whispered.

Pen touched Elinor's brow and the heat warmed her fingers.

Grace crawled over to look at Elinor. "See them red bumps on her neck? There's children with the same rash. Ship's fever, they call it." She wrapped her own ragged coverlet around Elinor.

"What can we do?" Pen asked.

"Nothing but wait," Grace replied.

"She won't die," Bram said fiercely.

"It's not for us to know God's will," Grace said.

"We'll all have it 'fore we're done," Rose said sharply, and backed away.

Elinor moved restlessly under the coverlet. "So cold," she whimpered. "Won't you build up the fire?"

"Rest easy," Bram murmured, stroking his sister's hair. "I'll build you a roaring fire, I will."

Pen and Bram stayed with Elinor all day and through the night. Toward dawn, they both slipped into exhausted sleep.

Pen awoke with a start when she felt a tug on her sleeve. She opened her eyes, to find Elinor's hand resting on her arm. Elinor was no longer shivering.

"You're better," Pen said.

"Bram," Elinor said softly.

Pen glanced at Bram, who was still asleep beside her. "Shall I wake him?" Pen asked eagerly. "He'll be so glad you're past the worst."

Elinor shook her head slightly. "Watch out for him," she said. "He's never been on his own."

Pen said quickly, "You'll be with him."

Elinor closed her eyes. Then she whispered, "Me gown."

"What?"

"Give it to Rose."

"I don't understand."

"She'll have a hard time in Virginia," Elinor said. It seemed to take all her strength to utter the words. "Dressed as she is, they'll think her a strumpet. Give her me gown. Promise."

"I promise," Pen said. "But you'll be here to care for us," she insisted. "As you've always been."

Elinor drifted into a placid sleep. As the first light of morning showed around the hatch door, she sighed. Then she was still.

Stiff and dry-eyed, Bram stayed with his sister's body all day. He refused to allow them to cover her face. In the afternoon, Pen sat down beside him.

"We must bathe her now," Pen said. "Go to the boys, Bram. They need you."

Bram stared woodenly at Elinor's face and said nothing.

"Jory's in a bad way," Pen said. Her voice choked and she swallowed. "No one can console him but you."

Rose came to sit with them. "There's nothing you can do here," Rose said to Bram. "Least you was with her when it mattered. Not like me—too afraid of the fever to be of comfort to her."

"It's always been Elinor and me," Bram said in an anguished voice. "Always there for each other. Now . . ." His eyes filled with tears. "Now, I'm truly an orphan."

"You have me," Rose said almost timidly. "And Pen, and the boys. We're your family, too."

Tears slid unnoticed down Pen's cheeks. "Come with me," she said, grasping his arm. "I'll take you to Jory."

While Bram talked to the boys, Pen and Grace bathed Elinor with rags torn from the coverlet. Rose sat close by, watching but not offering to help.

Pen glanced at Rose. "Elinor was out of her head," Pen said. "She didn't know who was with her."

"But I know," Rose replied.

"The fever scares us all," Grace said. "You'd be a fool not to be frightened."

"Not to be a coward, you mean," Rose said in a hard voice.

"We haven't time to mollycoddle you, Rose," Pen said. "Take off your gown."

Rose looked startled.

"She wanted you to have her gown," Pen said impatiently.

A low moan escaped from Rose's lips.

"That's all you can do for her now," Grace said gently. "Take the gift she offered."

It was near sunset when five of the ship's crew came below for Elinor and the bodies of three children who had died. Since they had no linen to wrap the bodies, the children were naked, their clothing saved for those who needed it more. Elinor was dressed in the black-and-crimson gown.

Passengers from below followed silently as the bodies were carried above deck. There were only the sounds of the wind and the sobbing of a mother to accompany the solemn procession.

The sailors carried their burdens to the rail and seemed ready to pitch them over without ceremony when Bram cried out, "A prayer! For cert there's someone who can offer a prayer for me sister and the little ones."

No one spoke for a moment. Then Grace said, "I'll say a prayer for these young ones. And may you do the same for me when my time comes."

She closed her eyes and began to speak.

Almighty God, we commend to You the souls
of our departed sisters and brothers: Elinor, Sarah,

John, and Davie, and we commit their bodies to the
sea, in sure and certain hope of the Resurrection
unto eternal life. Lord, take these children who
have walked the earth such a short time and
deliver them to the land of light and joy. And have
mercy on us who still carry our earthly burdens,
that we may at length follow these children to Your
side. The Lord gave, and the Lord hath taken
away. Blessed be the name of the Lord. Amen.

Pen and Rose stayed above deck with Bram until the moon began to rise. Even the ship's crew had pity for the mourners and didn't hurry them below.

Pen shivered in the cold wind. Her eyes felt gritty and tight from crying. She leaned against the rail and looked up at the sky. A full moon gleamed like a pewter plate caught in firelight, reminding Pen of her mother. The snow moon, Mam had called this first full moon of November. With winter coming, Mam would have been cutting wood and digging up the last of the potatoes. She would have been watching the moon for signs of winter gales.

"The water's so dark and cold," Bram said, his voice breaking. "I can't bear to think of her out there alone."

Rose put her arms around him. He buried his face in her hair and began to weep.

Pen wanted to go to him, but there seemed to be no place for her there. She crept away without Bram or Rose noticing.

* * *

Eleven more died the following week. It was Bram who said a prayer when the bodies of Grace and Edom were lifted to the rail and cast into the sea.

November 1627
Virginia

15

THE SHIP'S CREW NO longer seemed to care whether they stayed below or not. Pen spent most of her time above deck. The sounds and smells of sickness belowdecks had become unbearable. That was how she happened to be standing at the rail one morning when a sailor high up in the rigging shouted, "Land ahead!"

The day was gray and unusually cold for November. Many of the passengers stood on the main deck, shivering in their thin, ragged clothing. When they heard the seaman's cry, they rushed to the rail and strained to catch their first sight of Jamestown.

"I don't see land," a man grumbled.

"Just more water," another agreed.

Pen shared their disappointment. Although she feared what lay ahead, she was anxious to feel solid ground beneath her feet after two wretched months aboard the ship.

"Look there!" a woman cried.

Pen looked and saw a tree limb floating in the dark water. It was true, then. They were nearing land.

Pen found Bram standing with Jory and Thomas. Rose pushed her way through the crowd to join them. She looked different now, wearing Elinor's plain gown, her curls hidden beneath Elinor's cap. The paint was long gone from her lips, as was the sassy smile. Rose looked pale and solemn as they neared their destination.

"We may not have another chance to talk," Bram said quietly. "Just remember, if we're separated, I'll find you and get you away from this devilish place. I swear I will."

Rose nodded, her dark eyes fastened to Bram's face.

Pen couldn't bear to think of being separated from Bram. He made her feel stronger. Without him, she would be alone again. "And if they keep us in chains?" Pen asked, her voice strained.

"Then I'll break the chains," Bram said. He cupped her chin with his hand. "Have faith, dear heart," he said gently. "Do you not trust me to keep me promise?"

Pen's heart sped up at the touch of his hand. For an instant, she felt joy. Then their circumstances came back to her and she wanted to weep. "I trust you," she said.

Bram seemed unaware of the jealous glint in Rose's eyes, but Pen saw it. She looked away quickly, and her eyes fell on Jory. He was scowling, trying to appear brave. But his knuckles were white from gripping the rail so tightly. Beside him, Thomas looked grim.

It was late morning when a smudge of land came into view on the horizon. Everyone pressed against the rail, trying to see. Some of the women and children fell to their knees, weeping and offering prayers of thanksgiving.

"Is it Jamestown?" Bram asked a seaman who was hurrying past.

"Nay, that's Point Comfort," the sailor said, and was gone before Bram could ask more.

As the ship inched closer to Point Comfort, Pen could see the walls of a fort atop a bluff. A light fog over the water gave the fort a gray, ghostly appearance. Pen could just make out the lines of a wharf, where another ship was anchored, and a small boat was moving through the mist toward them.

Suddenly, sailors appeared with chains to shackle the men and boys.

"And where do you think we'd run to?" Bram demanded bitterly as the man locked iron rings around his wrists.

Pen watched the small boat approach the ship, and she wouldn't look at Bram. She couldn't stand to witness his shame. But Rose stared at the chains with fury in her eyes.

"Filthy swine," Rose muttered under her breath. "But you'll show 'em what's what."

"Aye," Bram said through clenched teeth. "I'll show 'em."

The boat had reached the ship. Sailors threw down a rope and pulled two men aboard. The ship's captain went to speak with them.

"We're bound for Jamestown," the captain said. "We've brought supplies and bondsmen."

One of the men stared at the people assembled on deck. Pen looked at her shipmates as this elegant

Englishman must see them: thin, ragged, drooping with hunger and sickness.

"A beggarly lot," the Englishman said.

Pen's cheeks burned. She reached for Bram's manacled hand. His strong fingers closed tightly around her own.

The ship sailed slowly up the James River. Dense forests of oak, pine, and cypress rose from its banks. This land seemed ominous to Pen. The silence was unearthly, and the immensity of the trees made her feel small and afraid. She wrapped her arms around herself, not knowing if she shivered more from cold or from apprehension.

Jamestown stood on a point of land that jutted into the river. Thatched roofs peeked over a high log wall. More buildings were scattered among the trees outside the fort, some of them whitewashed and standing a full two stories tall. Others were no more than hovels that appeared near collapse.

Pen and the others watched mutely as the ship pulled into a wharf at the base of the fort. The wall loomed over them, casting a deep shadow over the deck of the ship.

A crowd had gathered on the wharf. There were sailors from another ship, and those wearing the rough homespun of men and women who worked the land. But there were also men in gentleman's dress and women in fine wool cloaks and elegant bonnets like those Pen had seen in London. She didn't see anyone who looked like a savage, although she had no idea what a savage might look like.

A plank was lowered to the wharf, and the captain and some of the crew disembarked. Gentlemen shook the captain's hand and slapped him on the back, as if they knew him well.

While Pen and the others waited, the crew unloaded cargo from below: kegs of nails; rolled-up carpets; barrels of food, wine, and spices. By the time the belowdecks passengers were finally led down the plank, Pen was stiff with cold and weariness. With the men's chains clanking as they walked, the ship's crew herded them to one side of the wharf, the women and small children to the other.

Buyers began to walk past, studying them as they might examine sheep or oxen for sale. Pen moved close to Rose.

"Hold your head up," Rose hissed. "Don't let 'em know you're scared."

Pen lifted her chin and squared her shoulders, as she had seen Mam do all her life. She tried to look brave and proud.

16

PEN AND ROSE WATCHED as a man wearing a greasy wide-brimmed hat limped his way down the line of bondsmen and stopped in front of Bram. His dark hair bushed out from under the hat.

The man ran his hands down Bram's arms and legs. He pried open Bram's glaring mouth and peered at his teeth. After circling Bram and studying him from all angles, the man went to the captain and pulled cash from his pocket.

A sailor unlocked Bram's irons and held him while Bram's new master tied his hands with rope. Bram was pulled like a resistant calf across the wharf to a canoe made from a hollowed-out log. Rose turned away, her eyes suspiciously bright, but Pen watched the canoe move upriver until it was out of sight. When it disappeared around a curve in the riverbank, she took a step as though to follow it.

A young man in rough homespun bought Jory's and Thomas's indentures. He spoke with them a long time, gently, it seemed to Pen. The man didn't tie them with ropes. He walked between them to his boat, appearing to listen while they talked. Then Jory said something that made the man laugh. His arm slipped around the boy's shoulder and Jory smiled.

"He seems kind," Pen said.

"Here, he does," Rose said. "But who's to say once he's got 'em home?"

Pen said nothing, but she held on stubbornly to her feeling that the man would treat Jory and Thomas with kindness. She was still convincing herself of this when a man in a black coat and hat walked up to her. He was tall and lean, with a stern face and graying hair. His blue eyes were so pale, they appeared almost silver. Those eyes traveled from Pen's face down to her feet. Pen felt her cheeks grow warm.

"Are you in good health?" the man asked.

"Aye," Pen said.

"Obedient?"

Mam didn't always think so, Pen thought, but she replied, "Aye."

"My wife's in need of help with the house," the man said. "Have you ever cared for children?"

Pen's spirits rose. Working in the house was better than slaving in the fields. "I'm fond of children," she said.

The man hesitated, and Pen held her breath.

"All right, then," he said gruffly. "But I'll expect a good day's work from you. No lying or thievery, mind you."

"I don't lie," Pen said. "Nor steal, either."

"We'll see about that," he said. "Wait here until I come for you. I've another girl to find."

"Another girl?" Pen glanced at Rose, who was standing apart but watching them. "Would you consider taking me sister, then? She's a hard worker, she is, and honest, too."

"So you'd say," the man answered. Then he asked, "Which one's your sister?"

Pen pointed to Rose, who was staring coldly at the man. "There she is," Pen said. "That's Rose."

The man studied Rose. "Looks sullen to me," he said.

"It was a hard voyage, not one to put joy in your heart," Pen said truthfully. "But she's a good girl, Rose is."

The man walked over to Rose. "Your sister tells me you're a hard worker. Is that so?"

Rose gave Pen a quizzical glance, then looked back at the man. "It's true enough," Rose said.

"Then come along, the both of you."

Pen and Rose followed him to the captain, who addressed him as Mr. Frye and treated him with deference. While the captain and Mr. Frye talked, Rose whispered to Pen, "So I'm your sister now, am I?"

Pen shrugged. "You told Bram we was family."

"Well, your speaking up may be me salvation," Rose said with some of her old spirit, "or me undoing. Whatever happens, me life's in your hands."

Pen snorted. "In a pig's eye," she said.

A boy no older than Pen waited at Mr. Frye's boat. He grinned as Pen and Rose approached, his eyes lingering longer on Rose. "Me name's Jacob," he said.

"No time for socializing," the man said brusquely.

"Aye, Master Frye," Jacob said. But he seemed untroubled by his master's sharpness, Pen noticed, so he must not fear a beating.

She sat down beside Rose in the boat. Jacob untied the line and took up the oars.

As they made their way upriver, Pen studied Jacob. His homespun shirt and breeches were in good repair, as were his boots. And he didn't have the gaunt look of one who had been starved. Pen allowed herself a pinch of optimism. Perhaps servitude in the Frye household would not be as hellish as she had feared.

After a long silence, Master Frye said, "I treat my servants fairly, but I won't tolerate idleness. You'll be freed from your indenture in seven years. If you try to escape meantime, you'll be severely punished. Is that understood?"

"Aye," Pen said.

Rose's head dipped in a stiff nod.

They traveled several miles upriver, seeing no one in the dense forests that lined the banks. The only sign of habitation was the occasional dock, where a small boat or dugout canoe was tied. Finally, Jacob guided the boat to one of these docks and jumped out to tie it up.

Pen and Rose climbed from the boat and followed Master Frye up a steep path that wound through the trees. Pen glanced back once and saw Jacob sitting on the edge of the dock. He was swinging his feet and whistling softly.

When they were nearly at the top of the hill, the trees

thinned and Pen could see the house. It was two stories of plaster and timber, with a shingled roof. Smoke rose from a brick chimney at each end. Behind the house was an assortment of outbuildings; then open land that stretched to the horizon. One part was meadowland, where cows and horses grazed behind stacked-rail fencing. The rest was cleared for planting.

Master Frye led Pen and Rose to the kitchen yard behind the house. Two women came out to meet them. They were both tall and had chestnut hair peeking from under their caps. The older one held a sleeping baby. Master Frye introduced her as his wife.

Mistress Frye was much younger than her husband, and pretty, Pen thought, though she looked listless.

"Did they bring the carpet for the parlor?" she asked. "And the bolts of cloth?"

"In all probability," Master Frye said curtly. "I'm going back now for the food and wine."

"You'll ask about the carpet and cloth," his wife said anxiously.

"I'll ask," he said.

Mistress Frye watched him disappear around the corner of the house. Then she shifted her gaze to Pen and Rose, looking cross.

"What are your names?" she asked.

Pen told her.

Mistress Frye looked them over, frowning. "Why does he think I need *two* girls to stumble over?" she muttered. Then she glanced at the woman beside her. "This is

108

Mistress Amity, my sister. You'll take most of your orders from her."

Amity was no more than twenty, Pen guessed. Her face was too long and narrow to be called pretty, but her expression was lively and curious.

"You must be weary," Amity said, her dark eyes resting kindly on the girls. "And hungry, as well."

The baby began to cry. Mistress Frye looked down in bewilderment, as though she had no idea how to tend to a wailing infant.

Amity reached for the babe. "There now, Samuel," she crooned. "Hush, darling boy." She rocked him until he was quiet.

"Will you see to the children after their naps?" Mistress Frye asked Amity in a strained voice. "I must lie down until supper." She pressed her fingertips to her forehead. "This frightful headache."

"Of course," Amity said.

As Mistress Frye went inside, Amity turned to Pen and Rose.

"Come with me to the kitchen," she said, "and I'll see that you're fed."

17

HESTER, THE COOK, WAS tall and sturdy, with wisps of snowy hair and jowls that hung down over the collar of her homespun gown. She gave Pen and Rose a thorough going-over with her vivid blue eyes but didn't bother to respond when Amity introduced them.

"Sit," Hester said, and pointed to the table beside the hearth. She filled two earthenware bowls with porridge and set them on the table, along with a plate of bread that was yellow and grainy.

"This is corn pone made from Indian meal," Amity said, noticing Pen's stare. "Try some."

Pen reached for a square of bread and bit into it. The rich tastes of corn and butter filled her mouth.

Amity watched her, smiling. "Wait until you taste the fish that swim in these waters. And the mussels and oysters. We may be far from civilization, but our menus are more delightful than Londoners could imagine."

Pen gulped down her porridge. It was made with thick, sweet cream and tasted so good. When the bowls were empty, Hester filled them again. The worst of her hunger sated, Pen could eat less hurriedly now, taking time to savor each bite.

Hester was sprinkling a handful of dried herbs into a kettle on the hearth. She seemed to be a reticent woman, Pen thought, but not unkind.

Amity sat with them while they ate. She was anything but reticent herself, talking about everything imaginable while rocking the babe in her arms.

"I'm glad you're both here," Amity said finally. "One of you will clean and do washing and help with the children. There's baby Samuel here, and Dinah, who's four, and two-year-old Henry. The other will care for the animals and keep the barn clean. You can decide between yourselves who'll take which job."

"I don't know anything about livestock," Rose said quickly. "I'd be more help in the house."

Which was fine with Pen. Caring for the animals appealed to her more than sweeping floors and washing linens.

When they had finished eating, Amity took them up a narrow staircase to the bedchamber they would share with Hester. The room was bare except for three cots, a washstand, and a tall cupboard. Sunlight spilled through the lead-glass window, causing the pine floor to glow as yellow as a cat's eyes. Pen touched a blanket on one of the cots. It was thick and soft, like Mam's.

Amity opened the cupboard and brought out home-spun gowns, stockings, caps, and aprons.

"You can put these on," she said. "And here's a shawl for each of you, and a pair of shoes. Jacob made the shoes. If they don't fit, he can make more."

Pen breathed in the fresh scents of wool and linen that had been recently washed and dried in the sun. Even these smells reminded her of Mam. But then Pen thought of Bram and the little boys. Would they have a room and clothing this fine? Had they been welcomed with good food and encouraging words? The fear that they hadn't fared as well as she and Rose dulled Pen's pleasure.

"You can wash up there," Amity said, pointing to the washstand. "When you've changed and rested, I'll show you the house."

Next morning, Pen took the cattle and horses to graze in the meadow. She was scattering corn for the chickens when she heard the sound of hammering. Pen followed the sound with her eyes and saw Jacob straddling the high peak of the barn's roof. His hammer stopped in midair and he waved. Pen walked over to see what he was doing.

"There's a leak in the roof," he said when she asked him. "There wasn't time to mend it 'til the tobacco was brought in."

"That's what they grow in those fields?" Pen asked, looking out over the vast stretch of barren land.

"Aye, it's tobacco that makes a man rich in these colonies," Jacob said. "Once I'm free and have me own fifty acres, it's tobacco I'll be growing."

Pen squinted against the rising sun. "Seems like a lot of land for you to work alone."

"There were four bondsmen," he said, "but two died of the summer fevers and the other's term just ended. When the next ship comes in, we'll get more to replace 'em."

"Do many die?" Pen asked.

"Aye. Most of the lads that sailed with me three years ago are gone," Jacob said. "And the girl that cared for the livestock before you. Though Master Frye's servants do better than most. He's not so harsh, you see. But nothing can be done to stop the sickness when it comes."

The mention of harsh masters made Pen think of Bram and the boys.

"Jacob, there was a man buying servants at the wharf yesterday," she said. "He was dark-haired and walked with a limp."

"That would be Francis Cooper," Jacob said with a sneer. "Lives in a shack upriver, a stinking, filthy place it is. But it's a big plantation. They say he's making his fortune quick enough."

"What kind of master is he?"

"Terrible hard," Jacob said. "Flogs his servants for the sport of it, and I've seen the scars meself. There's talk he's buried more than one with his beatings."

Pen felt suddenly cold inside. She wrapped her arms around herself, but this brought no warmth or comfort. Bram might be in danger, even as she stood here talking with Jacob, and there was nothing she could do to stop it. And what of the little boys?

"There was another man," Pen said. "He was younger, wearing homespun. He seemed kindly, and he took two little boys. One with red hair."

Jacob nodded. "I seen 'em leave. That's Peter Bristol. He'll be good to the boys, him and Goody Bristol."

Pen was relieved to hear that. But there was still Bram. He wouldn't bow meekly to another man's will—even one who was searching for a reason to use his whip.

Jacob was staring down at her. "You look fair peaked," he said. "Are you not well?"

But Pen didn't hear him. She had already started back to the kitchen yard.

Pen labored from dawn to dark, but she was used to hard work and found it agreeable. Most of her day was spent outside, and that gave her a sense of freedom. She especially enjoyed the walks to and from the meadow with the livestock. It reminded her of home. Of Emma and Maud. And Mam.

At the end of the day, while Hester served the family supper in the hall, Pen and Rose took their meal in the kitchen. Sometimes Amity joined them.

"How did you happen to come to Virginia?" Pen asked Amity one evening.

"My sister has a delicate constitution," Amity said. "When Dinah was born, Rachel was too weak to care for her and asked that I come to help. It seemed a rare adventure, coming to the wilderness. I thought to return to England once Dinah was walking, but then Henry was born, and now Samuel." Amity smiled. "So four years later, here I still am."

"Will you go back to England when Samuel's older?"

Pen asked. She didn't like to think of Amity leaving.

"Mayhap," Amity replied thoughtfully.

"But not likely," Hester said, giving Amity a knowing look.

"Now, Hester," Amity said, her cheeks growing pink.

Pen looked from one to the other. She didn't understand what hidden meaning the exchange had for them, but it was clear that Hester was fond of Mistress Amity.

Rose ate her meal in silence, as she usually did. Pen rarely had a chance to speak with her alone, but she thought that Rose seemed content enough. Her thin face was filling out and her cheeks were a healthy pink—a far cry from the gaunt, painted face she had presented when Pen first met her. Gone were the sulky expression and sharp tongue, but Pen could sense a wariness in Rose. She didn't trust these people and their kindness.

Pen was uneasy with Master Frye, but she saw little of him. When he wasn't in the tobacco sheds with Jacob, he was off to Jamestown or at a neighbor's plantation. Nor did Pen see much of Mistress Frye, who sometimes spent entire days in her bedchamber with an aching head or palpitations in her chest. Pen couldn't decide if the woman's trouble was poor health or simply her disposition. It was plain enough that she wasn't happy, the way she stared out the window for hours at a time, apparently lost in sorrowful thoughts.

"Virginia must seem harsh to a lady as frail as Mistress Frye," Pen said to Amity.

"My sister misses our home in England," Amity

115

replied. "To see her now, you'd never believe how gay and lively she was as a girl."

Nay, Pen thought; she couldn't imagine that at all.

"But she was growing old, twenty-four and still unmarried," Amity said. "So many of the young men had died of the dark sickness, Rachel feared she'd end up a spinster. Then she heard they were asking for women to come to the colonies as wives."

"She came here to marry?" Pen asked in surprise.

"Six years ago," Amity said. "She was charming and pretty, and she caught Edward Frye's eye. He paid the one hundred and fifty pounds for her passage and took her for his bride."

Rose had given Amity her full attention. "You mean he bought her," Rose said, "as he did us."

Amity frowned. "It isn't the same thing at all," she said. "Gentlewomen were needed to civilize the colony. It was courageous of my sister to come here. But it's a hard life for someone like Rachel, who delights in parties and shopping and visiting with neighbors."

"And what of you?" Rose persisted. "Do you not miss England?"

"Not a whit," Amity said briskly. "As austere as our lives are here, I've found it rather to my liking."

"Even with the savages?" Rose demanded. "Don't you fear they'll kill you while you sleep?"

"I thought, mayhap, that you didn't speak at all," Amity said, sounding amused. "I realize now I was wrong. But to answer your question, we rarely see Indians these days. The year before I came, they attacked Jamestown and the nearby plantations, and many of the colonists were killed. But our people fought back, destroying the Indians' crops and burning their villages. It's been quiet for a while. Most of the Indians have moved away. Except the ones too old or infirm to leave. You needn't fear them, Rose."

"Even so," Rose said stubbornly, "there's nothing here but trees and water and silence. Not even an alehouse."

Amity smiled. "That's exactly what I like about it," she said.

18

"Pen, will you come here, please?" Amity called from the door of the spinning house.

Pen poured the last of the slop into the pigs' trough and started across the kitchen yard, clutching her shawl around her. A brisk wind blew, and Pen was happy enough to get in out of the cold.

When Pen entered the little house used for spinning and sewing, she saw that Rose was there, wearing a new gown of blue wool. Amity squatted at Rose's feet, turning up the hem and pinning it.

"That should do," Amity said. She stood up and saw Pen. "Here, my girl, try these on." She handed Pen a gown made from the same blue wool, a heavy cloak, and a nightdress.

Pen appeared dazed. "These are for me?"

"They are," Amity said.

"You sewed them yourself?"

"Every stitch."

"But *why*?" Pen exclaimed.

Amity laughed. "Because, silly goose, you and Rose need warm clothing for the winter. Now, put on the gown so I can pin the hem."

Pen took off her gray homespun and slipped the wool gown over her head. It felt soft against her skin. She held out the skirt to admire it.

"Rose," Pen asked, "have you ever seen such a fine gown?"

"I had a satin gown once," Rose said, looking at Amity. The memory seemed to make her sad. "It was black, with a crimson petticoat."

And it was stained and torn, Pen wanted to say, and you were too bony for it because there was never enough to eat.

"We haven't much use for satin gowns here," Amity said kindly.

But on Sunday morning, Mistress Frye and Amity came to the dock wearing silk gowns that whispered when they walked. Mistress Frye's was green and Amity's was lavender. The skirts were so full beneath their wool cloaks, the women had to gather them up to climb into the boat and sit down.

Pen saw the envious look Rose gave the women. Pen herself had no desire for silk dresses. Her wool gown pleased her well enough.

No one spoke until they neared the Jamestown wharf. Then Master Frye looked at Pen and Rose and said, "I trust you will conduct yourselves with piety and humility. My servants' behavior reflects on me."

Rose lowered her head in a gesture that others might take for acquiescence. But Pen saw the flush of anger in her cheeks.

They entered the stockade and walked a short way to the church house. The Frye family sat up front with the other important families. Pen and Rose followed Hester to a bench at the back.

Pen caught sight of the back of Bram's head and nudged Rose to point him out.

"Can you see his face?" Rose whispered. "Does he look well?"

"I can't tell."

Hester gave them a sharp look and Pen settled down. But her eyes wandered across the congregation until she found Jory's bright head. Thomas sat beside him. Peter Bristol and a young woman were on the other side of Jory. The woman leaned down to whisper something to Jory. When he lifted his face to nod, Pen saw that he looked content.

The Reverend Tobias Reed stepped to the front of the church. He was a small man, but he seemed larger when he began to speak. Indeed, his voice filled the room to the rafters when he bellowed, "If sinners entice thee, consent thou not! If they say to you, 'Come with us, cast in thy lot with us,' refrain from joining them on their path. For they are evil and they lurk privily for the innocent among us!"

He speaks only of evil, Pen thought, never of kindness and mercy. She was glad when the long sermon ended and the preacher led them in prayer.

Pen hoped to have a word with Bram after the

service. She saw him coming down the aisle, his eyes searching the faces around him. Pen started toward him, but a knot of women blocked her path. As he passed their bench, Bram spotted Pen and Rose. His face lit up and he stopped. Pen raised her hand in greeting. But Francis Cooper came and shoved Bram toward the door. By the time Pen and Rose left the church, Mr. Cooper was already herding his bondsmen to the wharf. Pen could have wept with disappointment.

While the Fryes visited with friends in the churchyard, Pen stood with Rose and Hester. Pen listened with growing despair to the talk of sickness and death. She was relieved when she saw Amity coming.

But Amity paused before she reached them, seeming to search the ground for something she had lost. Nearby was a tall, well-dressed man who would have been handsome but for the deep pockmarks that scarred his face. Several male servants waited while he talked with neighbors. Pen noticed one of the servants moving closer to Amity. Pen was startled when she saw him reach for Amity's hand. Amity didn't look up from the ground, but she gripped the man's hand tightly.

It was over in an instant. Amity moved away. The young man's eyes followed her. Amity's cheeks were still pink when they left the stockade for the boat.

After dinner, Pen looked out the window and saw Amity sitting on the hill that overlooked the river. Baby Samuel was in her arms, and Dinah and Henry played nearby. Pen changed to her everyday dress and went to join them.

Dinah had placed her dolls around a low tree stump. She was serving them mud pies on pieces of bark and acorn caps filled with seeds. Henry tossed pinecones at his sister and crowed with delight when they landed on the dolls' table, sending mud pies and acorn tops flying.

"Henry! Stop that!" Dinah placed her hands on her hips and glared at her brother. "You've ruined the children's supper!"

Henry gave her a devilish grin and threw another pinecone.

Pen sat down beside Amity, dead leaves crunching as she settled herself on the ground. Through the bare branches of oaks and chestnut trees, she could see the James River sparkling in the November sun. Amity was gazing at the river with a look of contentment.

She glanced at Pen, then looked back at the river. "Virginia's a beautiful land, isn't it? Not all tidy like our little towns and fields in England, but rather grand in its own way."

"Aye," Pen said. "I found Virginia frightening at first, but I've grown to like it."

"You'll like it more in the spring, when the dogwoods bloom and the trees are filled with songbirds. And less in summer." Amity made a face. "The heat can be terrible, and we're plagued with mosquitoes."

They sat in silence while Pen tried to think of a way to find out about the man who had held Amity's hand. Finally, she said, "There was a gentleman in church today. He was tall and had pockmarks on his face."

"What about him?"

"I just wondered who he was," Pen said casually. "He must be very rich to have so many servants."

"His name is Richard Galthorpe," Amity said. "He has a large plantation downriver."

"Is he a good master?"

Amity looked quizzically at Pen. "Quite good," she said. "He's a decent man. But why do you ask?"

"No reason," Pen said.

"Didn't Rose want to come outside?" Amity asked.

"She's resting." Pen had left Rose lying on her cot, staring at the ceiling. No doubt she was thinking about Bram, although she never spoke of him. Pen was sure Rose thought about Bram every day, as she did herself. Most nights Pen lay awake, wondering if Bram was well, if Francis Cooper fed him enough, if he was being worked too hard. She wondered, too, if Bram ever thought about her. It was troubling to speculate on whether he might be injured or hungry, but it was comforting, as well, to drift into sleep with Bram there in her thoughts.

"She isn't happy here, your sister," Amity remarked. She reached for Pen's hand and studied the palm. "Your hands are callused from hard work, but Rose's are smooth." There were questions in her eyes.

Pen looked away. She had forgotten telling Master Frye that Rose was her sister.

"You don't look anything alike," Amity said.

"We're not sisters. I just said we were so Master Frye would bring her here."

Pen was surprised that Amity didn't seem upset by the lie.

"Rose is me friend," Pen said in explanation. "I didn't want to be alone."

"I see," Amity said. Then: "Tell me about your life in England. Do you have family there? Is there someone you miss?"

"Nay," Pen said. "Me mother died in April. I never knew me father—he died before I was born."

"Did you and your mother live in London?"

"I've only been to London three times in me life. We lived in a small village." Pen didn't tell Amity how the villagers had turned their faces away when she and Mam walked past. "We had our cottage, and two goats named Maud and Emma. Mam grew herbs, and took bread and goat cheese to London to sell."

"You were happy," Amity said. "You had a good mother."

Pen wasn't sure about being happy. Life in the village had always been hard. But she had no doubts at all about her mother, and so she nodded.

"What happened to her?" Amity asked. "Do you mind my asking?"

Pen found that she didn't mind. She was ready to talk about her mother's death. And everything that had happened since.

"There was a storm," Pen said. "I went to bring the goats home from the high meadow, but the ravine behind our cottage filled with water. I fell in; I was drowning. Mam came after me. Someone dragged me out of the water, but they didn't save her."

"Oh, Pen," Amity said. "I'm so sorry."

Pen felt tears gathering behind her eyes. This will never do, she told herself sternly. She took a deep breath.

"Was there anyone to take care of you?" Amity asked.

"An old couple in the village took me in." Pen was surprised at how angry she still felt when she thought of Hugh and Sarah Alwin. "They took the goats, and some of Mam's things. I stayed 'til I paid them off; then I left for London. That's where I met Rose and—and others, who made their living playing music and singing and juggling."

"Street performers," Amity said. "But where did you live?"

"In the cellars of an empty house."

"That must have been awful."

Pen shook her head. "It was rather comfortable," she said, "but then the spirits came. Late one night. They broke into the cellars and dragged us off to the gaol."

Amity looked horrified. "Who are these spirits you speak of?"

"They're paid to steal children who can be shipped to Virginia as indentured servants."

Amity was shaking her head in disbelief. "You must be . . . mistaken."

"Nay, I'm not," Pen said firmly. "I was there! I know what they did. They tied us up and took us to Bridewell. We stayed in the gaol through the summer, 'til there was a ship leaving for Virginia. Some died of gaol fever"—Pen thought of Kitty, and then her mind shifted to Elinor—"and others died on the voyage. We were crammed in

125

belowdecks, either burning up or freezing to death, and always hungry."

Pen stopped—to catch her breath, to think about what she had said—and expected Amity to speak. But there was only silence. Pen wondered if she had said something wrong, something to offend Amity. She looked up and saw the distress—nay, the *anger*—in Amity's face, and she wished fervently that she hadn't spoken at all.

"This . . . *spiriting*," Amity said carefully. "It must have happened before. You and Rose wouldn't have been the first."

Pen sensed now that Amity believed her, and that she was angry not at Pen, but at those who had been party to abducting her. "We weren't the first," Pen said. "In the gaol, they spoke as if it happened all the time."

Amity sighed. She slipped an arm around Pen's shoulders. When Pen looked into her face, she saw that there was no anger left. Only caring.

Pen settled into the crook of Amity's arm, and they gazed at the river together.

19

As CHRISTMASTIDE DREW NEAR, Rose spent long hours in the kitchen helping Hester bake pies and custards. Pen's teeth chattered when she milked the cows on these cold mornings, and she envied Rose her place beside the warm hearth.

Pen tried not to think about the approach of Christmas, because she couldn't imagine the day without her mother. But one crisp, bright morning, as she herded the cows and horses toward the meadow, Pen was reminded of other such mornings when she had left the cottage with Maud and Emma, and Mam had asked her to bring back greenery. Mam would hang ivy around the door and fill the milk pitcher with holly sprigs—laughing every time they needed to pour up milk and had no place to pour it. For Christmas dinner, they would have a bit of fresh fish with their bread and cheese, and sometimes plum pudding, if Mam had had a good week at Cheapside. While the villagers had filled the church with hymns and piety, Pen had listened to her mother's stories. It was the one day of the year when Mam had time to summon up memories from her youth and share them with her daughter. Christmas would never be the same now.

The frost-covered grass crunched under Pen's shoes as she followed behind the animals. Jacob and Master Frye's two new bondsmen were already out mending fences. Master Frye was there, as well, watching the work from atop his fine-boned chestnut mare.

The new servants looked strong, but they were young—no more than twelve or thirteen.

"That rail's knotted!" Master Frye shouted. "It won't hold."

The new boys lowered the offending rail to the ground and scurried for a different one.

Pen glanced at Master Frye's dour face while she waited for the livestock to pass through the gate. He looked as though no fence rail in the world would ever please him.

When Pen came back from the meadow, she threw down grain for the chickens and gathered the eggs. Hester and Rose were up to their elbows in dough when Pen took the eggs to the kitchen house.

"I can't spare Rose to take Mistress her tea," Hester said. She wiped her face on her sleeve. "Pour a cup for her and one for Mistress Amity," she said to Pen. "But wash the smell of cow off 'fore you take it to 'em."

When Pen entered the house with the tea tray, she heard women's voices coming from down the hall. She moved slowly toward the voices, being careful to hold the tray balanced so the tea wouldn't slop over. She was nearly to the end of the hallway when she heard weeping.

"Hush, Rachel," Amity was saying. "It's not as bad as you think."

"It's every bit as bad," Mistress Frye said through her tears. "The house isn't kept to his liking, and he claims he can't hear himself think for the children's noise. I tell him children will make noise, but he says if I were a proper mother, I'd keep them quiet and tidy."

Pen had reached the open door to the great room. Mistress Frye was sitting in a high-backed chair near the hearth. Amity stood nearby.

"Edward's right," Mistress Frye said. She dabbed at her eyes with a handkerchief. "I'm not a proper mother, nor wife, either. It's impossible here, with dirt tracked in all day and no decent help. Do you remember all the servants Mother had?" she asked wistfully. "How they kept the floors shining and the house smelling so sweet? These rough floors will never shine," she said bitterly, "and the house will always smell of animal dung."

"Rachel—"

"I so detest it here!" Mistress Frye wailed. "How does he expect our children to behave properly when they're growing up in this heathen place?"

"Rachel, must you break into tears every day?" Amity said wearily. "Tell Edward he should be grateful his children are healthy enough to whoop and holler."

"You don't understand," Mistress Frye said. "How can you, with no husband of your own?"

Amity saw Pen standing at the door. "Time for your tea, Rachel," she said.

"Even the tea is dreadful," Mistress Frye sniffed. "Why did I ever come to this godforsaken place?"

Francis Cooper wasn't at church for two Sundays. But on Christmas Day, he showed up with his servants in tow as the Reverend Reed began his sermon. Pen thought it odd that Bram didn't look for her and Rose, but kept his eyes to the floor. Then she saw the ugly bruise on his cheekbone and the way he limped down the aisle.

Pen leaned forward to see him better.

"God's blood," Rose whispered. "He's been beat."

Hester gave each a look that was supposed to make them grow still and listen to the sermon, but for once, the look failed. Pen didn't care what the minister was saying. All she could think about was Bram. Her eyes didn't move from his bowed head until the service was over, and people stood up and blocked her view. Then Pen leaped to her feet, earning another glare from Hester.

Pen was finally able to see Bram close-up when Francis Cooper herded his bondsmen to the door. She caught her breath at the sight of Bram's swollen, discolored face. His lip was torn and there was a nasty cut above his eye. Pen pictured fists pounding his face, over and over, and Bram unable to defend himself. The image left her weak. She had to do something! But *what*?

Hester had grabbed Pen's arm and was shoving

her toward the aisle. "Be quick," Hester said. "I've a Christmas dinner to finish."

They walked out of the shadowy church into a harsh light that hurt Pen's eyes. She followed Hester and Rose to the boat, thinking that this was a miserable Christmas Day. The worst of her life.

Hester served a feast: turkey and rockfish; baked Indian bread with fresh butter and honey; poke sallet with vinegar and acorn oil; berry pies and baked custard and cranberry tarts. But Pen had no appetite.

Rose glanced at Pen's barely touched plate and helped herself to another slice of turkey. When Hester left them to serve the Fryes their dessert, Rose said, "Starving yourself won't help him."

Pen ate a few bites and pushed the rest of the food around on her plate.

Rose reached for Pen's bread. "If you're not going to eat it . . ." she said.

The way Rose was cramming food down her gullet made Pen feel queasy.

"Winter's not the time to escape," Rose said, chewing and thinking. "We'll wait for spring. If Bram can't come to us by then, we'll go to him."

"What if he doesn't make it 'til spring?"

Rose glared at her. "Bram's strong. You don't know him as I do."

"Mayhap Mistress Amity could help us," Pen said. "If we told her how Bram's master beats him—"

"Are you rattlebrained?" Rose demanded. "Your sweet little Amity's no different from the rest. Do you

131

think she'd care a whit what happens to a bondsman?"

Pen didn't answer. But a few days later, she learned that Amity had reason to care very much what happened to a bondsman.

Pen was sweeping the kitchen yard with a brush broom when a man leading a horse approached the back of the house. Pen recognized the man at once. It was the servant who had held Amity's hand that Sunday in the churchyard.

The man was tall, with sandy-colored hair that fell across his eyes. He smiled at Pen.

"Fair morn, missy," he said. "Can you tell me where I'd find Jacob?"

Pen pointed toward the barn. She knew she shouldn't stare, but she couldn't curb her curiosity. He stared back, amusement in his blue eyes.

"I see you're not one to jabber," he said. "But have you time to tell me your name?"

Pen felt her cheeks grow warm.

"I'm called Win. Winsome Fielding. And you're . . ."

"Pen Downing," she mumbled.

He grinned at her. "It's me pleasure to make your acquaintance, Pen Downing." Then he started for the barn.

Pen watched as Jacob came out and greeted the man. Jacob seemed glad to see him. The stranger noticed Pen watching, and waved.

Pen spun around and trotted back to the kitchen house.

When she came outside again, Jacob and Win were gone. But as Pen approached the barn, she heard Win's voice inside. Mayhap he is helping Jacob stable the horse, she thought. Pen opened the door a crack and was shocked to see that it wasn't Jacob, but Amity, who stood with Win beside the mare's stall. Win was rubbing the horse's ear and not looking at Amity.

"I've tried to find a reason to come," Win said. He glanced at Amity, then dropped his eyes again. "For cert, I'm grateful to Master Galthorpe for trading this little mare."

Amity smiled shyly at him. "So am I," she said.

"I'm getting the fifty acres on the bluff."

"Oh, Win, can you believe it's finally happening?" Amity sounded breathless.

"Me indenture will be up in two months' time," Win said. "Then I'll build the house. It won't be grand like the Fryes'—not at first. But we'll add on. One day, you'll have the finest house on the James River."

"I don't care about a fine house," Amity said.

"We'll build the house on the highest point," he said. "You'll be able to see every ship that sails up and down the river."

Then Win leaned toward Amity, and Pen realized he was going to kiss her. Pen jerked back from the door. She was astonished that a gentlewoman would consider marrying a bondsman. Mistress Frye must not know, Pen thought; otherwise, Amity and Win wouldn't be forced to meet in the barn.

Pen walked slowly to the kitchen yard. She was worried. If Amity left, who would run the house? For cert, Mistress Frye couldn't do it. And more importantly, Pen wondered, who will look out for Rose and me?

20

"ROSE, *LOOK*!"

Pen ran to the window, barefoot and shivering in her nightdress. The window was etched with frost like fine embroidery.

Rose slid from under her blanket and came to the window. Outside, the first rays of sun spread a yellow glow across the snow-covered hill. When Rose saw the snow, she smiled.

Pen and Rose dressed and hurried down the stairs to the kitchen. Hester already had bread baking.

"It snowed last night!" Pen exclaimed.

"Aye, and won't it make your work that much harder," Hester said.

But Pen didn't mind. She loved the snow. She loved how it made dull fields look beautiful, and how it glittered in the sun. She loved its hush, and its whispers when the wind blew.

Pen draped her cloak around her shoulders and pulled up the hood. Rose stood at the door, looking wistful, as Pen left for the barn.

Snow had drifted along the edges of the kitchen garden. Pen walked briskly, swinging her arms and breathing in the cold, clean air. No one else was out this early, and the only sound she heard was the sharp crunch of snow beneath her feet.

Then, suddenly, a figure appeared. It stepped from the poultry house, and stared straight at Pen.

Pen stopped short. This person wrapped in skins and fur was no one she knew. The face was dark and thin, the gray hair very long. Through her shock, Pen realized that she must be seeing her first Indian.

Pen's impulse was to scream and run back to the kitchen house. But she hesitated, unable to tear her eyes away from the peculiar figure. It was a woman, Pen decided. She was bent with age and clutching two eggs to her chest.

Still watching Pen, the old woman walked slowly toward the open fields. She had as much reason to be afraid as Pen, perhaps more, but Pen sensed no fear in the woman, only wariness. Pen started again for the barn. She didn't look back until she reached the door. The woman was gone.

Amity was in the kitchen when Pen came inside for supper. Hester was serving up hot venison stew.

"Your cheeks are red," Amity said when she saw Pen. "Come sit by the fire and thaw out."

Pen took off her cloak and sat down on a stool beside the hearth. She pulled off her wet shoes and stockings and spread them across the bricks to dry.

Amity handed her a bowl of stew. "I'll make you a hot posset with a drop of wine before bed to stave off a chill."

"She looks all right to me," Rose said, frowning into her stew.

Amity gave Rose a thoughtful look but said nothing. Pen knew that Rose envied her for what she considered a day spent frolicking in the snow. But there had been little time for play, and Pen was tired. She yawned as she ate the spicy stew. Then she remembered the Indian woman and came awake.

"I saw a savage today," she said.

All faces turned to her. Rose looked startled and Amity curious. Hester's face showed no emotion at all.

"You saw a savage and you're just thinking to tell us?" Rose asked. "Where was he? What did he look like?"

"It was an old woman," Pen said. "She was stealing eggs from the poultry house."

Hester clicked her teeth and scowled. "Back to their thievery, are they?"

"She only took two." Pen was thinking that it took more than that for one of Hester's rich custards.

"I used to see Indians once in a while," Amity said, "but it's been a long time now."

"If I never see one of their heathen selves again, it'll be too soon," Hester said vehemently. "You weren't here to witness what they did, Mistress Amity. Slaughtered babies in their cradles, they did." Hester closed her eyes, as if shutting out the memory of that day.

"It must have been horrible," Amity said. "But I don't think we need worry about Indian attacks anymore. The woman Pen saw may be the last one left."

Pen recalled the old woman's wariness, and the slowness with which she moved. It was hard to think of her as someone to fear.

The next morning, Amity dressed Dinah and Henry in their heaviest clothing and told Rose that she needed her help. Pen was feeding the chickens when she saw Rose and Amity bring the children outside. Amity pulled Henry on a small sled. Rose and Dinah scooped up handfuls of snow. When Rose turned her back, Dinah pelted her with snowballs. Rose laughed and shouted, "You little scamp!"

Rose lifted Dinah from the ground. The child shrieked with delight as Rose spun her around.

"Me, too! Me, too!" Henry screamed, stretching out his arms to be picked up.

Rose set Dinah down and reached for Henry.

Pen stood still, watching. Rose twirled across the snowy lawn with Henry in her arms. He giggled, and so did Rose. Imagine that, Pen thought, Rose giggling. Rose *happy*. In all the time she had known the girl, Pen had never seen her like this. The Rose that Pen had met on a gray street in London would never have lost herself in play.

Pen started for the kitchen house, smiling. Rose's laughter followed her.

21

"YOU'RE SHIRKING YOUR DUTY. It's *your* job to mind the children!"

Pen heard Mistress Frye's querulous voice as she entered the kitchen for her midday meal. The mistress and Amity were there, along with Hester. Mistress Frye was dipping a long-handled spoon into the stew pot.

"Have you come to think of me as your servant now?" Amity asked her sister.

"Don't be foolish." Mistress Frye bristled. She brought the spoon to her lips and tasted the stew. "Hester, this needs salt. You know how the master complains when it's tasteless."

Hester grunted and didn't bother to look up from the potatoes she was peeling.

"I thought Rose was brought here to care for the children," Amity said.

"I never agreed to that," Mistress Frye responded. "It's dangerous enough having bonded servants in my house, without leaving the raising of my children to them. I can only imagine their backgrounds."

"Rachel!" Amity glanced at Pen, then gave her sister a severe look.

"Well, it's true," Mistress Frye said defensively. "That girl has my babies wallowing on the ground like rooting hogs and screaming like savages. I don't want her caring for them."

"They love Rose," Amity said. "Is that what bothers you, Rachel?"

Color rose in Mistress Frye's cheeks. "That's enough!" she exclaimed. "I don't want that girl near my children, and that's that. If you defy me, I'll have to speak to Edward."

"And what will Edward do?" Amity demanded. "Send me back to England on the first ship? I think not. Edward's not one to discharge free labor."

"How trying you've become," Mistress Frye said in a cold voice. "Perhaps it *is* time to send you home."

"And leave you to care for your own children?" Amity snapped.

Mistress Frye gave her a furious look and hurried from the kitchen house.

Pen hung her cloak on the wall peg, watching Amity pace back and forth before the fire. Pen had never seen the woman this angry.

Amity said, "I apologize for my sister."

"Rose would never harm the children," Pen said.

"Of course she wouldn't! Anyone with eyes can see how much she loves them."

"Amity?"

"Hmm?" Amity didn't appear to be listening.

"They won't really send you away, will they?"

Amity's face lost its distracted look. She laughed softly. "Have no fear, pet," she said. "Once my sister has time to think, she'll be no more inclined to lose free labor than my brother-in-law would."

After that, Pen noticed that Rose was spending more time in the kitchen and less with the children. But whenever a new snow fell, Rose would be outside romping with Amity, Dinah, and Henry. Once, Pen saw Mistress Frye standing at the window, watching them play. But Pen heard no more about sending Amity back to England.

Francis Cooper made certain that no one approached his bondsmen, but Pen could still see Bram in church on Sundays and reassure herself that he was healing. Outwardly at least. By the time January gave way to February, Bram's battered face had mended and he no longer limped. But he was thin and pale, and Pen worried. So many in the community were ill. The Reverend Reed could barely make himself heard—with his booming voice—over the fits of coughing in the church house. A great number were too weak to leave their beds at all. Pen feared that in his run-down condition, Bram would fall victim to the sickness.

But illness was to come closer to home. Pen awoke one night to the sound of Hester's raspy cough. Crawling from her nest of blankets, Pen scurried across the cold floor to see about her. Hester's face was hot to the touch and she tossed fitfully. Having seen how swiftly a fever could ravage the body, Pen ran for Amity.

Amity sat with Hester all night, sending Pen to brew tea and to bring cold cloths. In the morning, Amity said to Pen, "Her fever's down, but she'll need a long rest to recover. Rose will have to take over the cooking. Help her as much as you can, won't you?"

A few days later, Winsome Fielding came to the house again. Pen was leaving the barn when she saw Amity running to meet him behind the poultry house. Win pulled Amity to him and they kissed. Rose was carrying a pail of vegetable peelings to the pigs' trough. When she saw Amity in the arms of a young man, she seemed to forget all about the pigs and rushed back to the kitchen house.

The first thing Rose said when Pen returned to the kitchen was, "Mistress Amity has a lover. I saw 'em snuggling behind the poultry house."

"Aye, they plan to marry," Pen said. She didn't like to think about it.

Rose's brows shot up in surprise. "For true? Well, tell me all you know," she demanded. "From the looks of him, he's not a gentleman."

"He's indentured," Pen said. "But his term's over soon."

"No wonder they meet in secret," Rose murmured. "She's not very pretty, but I'll wager her dowry's handsome enough. She wouldn't have to settle for the likes of him in England."

"I don't think she considers it *settling*," Pen said. "He's building her a house upriver."

"A hovel, I expect," Rose said with a sneer.

Pen was helping Rose prepare the midday meal when Amity swept into the kitchen. Mistress Frye was on her heels.

"We *will* talk about this," the mistress was saying. "Come back inside."

"There's nothing more to say," Amity said. "Rose, will you heat up the gruel for Hester?"

"Forget the gruel!" Mistress Frye's expression was anxious as she peered at her sister. "Do you know what Edward will say if he finds out about you and this servant?"

Amity's eyes flashed. "I don't *care* what Edward will say. Edward has nothing to do with me."

Suddenly, Mistress Frye startled them all by bursting into tears. "Amity, whatever are you thinking? This man isn't a fit husband for you."

"Rachel, he's the finest man I know."

"But he has nothing."

"He has fifty acres," Amity said. "And soon he'll build our house. What more do I need?"

"He has no money, no position."

"Like Edward, you mean." Amity frowned. "Have your husband's money and position made you happy?"

Mistress Frye couldn't have looked more shocked.

Amity sighed. "I'm sorry, Rachel, I shouldn't have said that. But you might as well accept the fact that I'm going to marry Win."

Mistress Frye looked pale. And defeated, Pen thought.

"Very well," the mistress said stiffly. "It's your life, and you don't need my permission to ruin it."

"You're quite right," Amity said cheerfully. "I don't."

"But don't expect my blessing," Mistress Frye warned. "I'm sure I don't know what I'll tell Edward."

"Tell him that I'm marrying the man I love."

Mistress Frye shot her an angry look. "He won't take it well."

"Then tell him it's none of his concern," Amity said. "I don't care what Edward thinks," she said more gently, "but I do want *you* to be happy for me, Rachel."

"You really love this man?" Mistress Frye's voice held a note of uncertainty.

"With all my heart," Amity said.

22

PEN BALANCED THE TRAY against her hip and opened the door. Hester was sitting up in bed and Amity was perched beside her.

"I should be in the kitchen," Hester grumbled. "No telling what these girls are feeding you."

"We've not been poisoned yet," Amity said cheerfully.

"I've only scorched the porridge twice," Pen said.

Hester scowled.

Amity took a cup of tea from the tray and handed it to Hester. "I'll be leaving next month," she said.

"To marry that boy?" Hester asked gruffly.

Amity nodded.

"The mistress can't be pleased," Hester said.

"She isn't."

"And the master?"

"I take it he doesn't approve," Amity said.

"Aye, and don't I believe that!"

"My sister spoke with him," Amity said. "He's accepted that he has no say in what I do."

145

Not wishing to hear any more about Amity's marriage, Pen started for the door. She didn't want Amity to leave, and she didn't like Win Fielding one bit for taking her away.

But there is nothing I can do to change it, Pen thought as she trudged down the stairs. Amity's mind was made up. And who could blame her for wanting to leave her helpless sister and ill-tempered brother-in-law? With Amity gone, Pen wished that *she* could flee this house, as well. And mayhap she would. When she and Rose found Bram, they would all be leaving Jamestown together.

It lifted Pen's spirits to imagine being with Bram again. She would take him nourishing food to build up his strength before the journey. She would make him laugh, and watch as he shed that look of despair. Then Pen's daydream became vague. She didn't want to dwell on how they would make their way through an uncharted wilderness and then endure another long voyage across the sea. She skipped over that part to when they would be in London again. She tried to forget the noise and the dirt and the hiding underground. They would still have to hide—and live in even greater fear of being hauled back to Bridewell. But what ties do I have to Virginia? Pen asked herself. There was only Amity who seemed to care, and Amity was going away.

England, on the other hand, was home. Pen had lived her entire life there. Her mother and father were buried in British soil. And in London, Pen would have Bram and

Rose, who were as close to being family as anyone still living. Why, Bram had helped her—mayhap saved her life!—when she was no more than a stranger. Didn't she owe him for that? And didn't he make her feel safe and happy when she was with him? Elinor had asked Pen to watch out for Bram, and so she would.

Mistress Frye had asked Goodwife Fletcher, the best seamstress in Jamestown, to make Amity's wedding gown. Pen was sweeping the hall when Goody Fletcher came for the final fitting. Pen followed the women to the door of the small parlor to watch.

Amity stood on a stool in the pale blue gown while Goody Fletcher tucked and pinned.

"There's a wrinkle across the bodice," Mistress Frye said, "and the skirt dips in front."

"Rachel," Amity said in gentle reproof.

"I only want your gown to be perfect."

"Give me time and it will be," Goody Fletcher snapped.

Mistress Frye circled Amity, looking critically at the gown. "Mother's pewter goblets will be my gift to you," she said.

"That's kind of you, Sister, but I wonder if I might ask for something else."

Mistress Frye was taken aback. "I thought you'd be pleased with the goblets!"

"They're lovely," Amity said, "but what I really need is help starting out in a new home. There's the garden to plant and linens to weave, candles to make—so many chores!"

Mistress Frye eyed her suspiciously. "What are you leading up to?"

"What I would like for a wedding gift are Pen's and Rose's indentures."

Pen gripped the broom handle to steady herself.

Mistress Frye gaped at her sister in stunned silence. Then she exploded. "You can't be serious! Edward would never agree."

"He would if you tell him that's what you want to do," Amity said.

"He'll say you're impossibly greedy," Mistress Frye said. "After he's given you a home these past four years—"

"After I've given him my labor," Amity corrected. "Surely that's worth more than a few pewter goblets."

"I'm shocked by your ingratitude!"

Mistress Frye glared at her sister, and from her perch on the stool, Amity glared back. Goody Fletcher squatted on the floor at Amity's feet, trying to ignore the battle that raged over her head.

"You don't trust the girls with your spoons, much less your children," Amity said. "How will it be when I'm not here to watch over them?"

"But Edward—"

"Fie on Edward!"

Pen backed away from the door and ran for the kitchen house.

"Rose!" Pen pushed open the door. "You'll not believe it!"

Rose didn't bother to look up from the pudding she was stirring. "If it's her ladyship's gown you've come to tell me about, I'm not interested," she said.

"Must you always be so grumbly?"

"And why not?" Rose demanded. "I slave for 'em from dawn to dark, and all the mistress does is whine and complain. I hate this house!"

"That's what I came to tell you. We may not be in this house much longer."

Rose's head shot up. "What are you saying?"

"Amity wants to take us," Pen said. "She's asked Mistress Frye for our indentures."

Rose's shoulders sagged. "Is that all?" she said, and turned back to the pudding.

"Don't you see? We'd be away from Mistress Frye and her whining. I know you'd miss the children—"

"I'd miss nothing," Rose said.

"Then wouldn't you rather be with Amity?"

"Bondage is bondage," Rose said. "I want nothing but to go back to London."

"We don't know that we'll ever get back."

"Then I'll die trying," Rose snapped.

"I think," Pen said slowly, "that we should look at this without sentiment. It wasn't always so good in London—was it? Living in cellars and never having enough to eat."

"At least I was free," Rose said stubbornly.

"Nay, you were in hiding," Pen said. "You lived underground like an outlaw."

Rose's eyes narrowed. "If Bram came for us today, would you go with him, or would you stay with your precious Amity? Now that you know she wants you, you aren't thinking of him at all!"

"That's not true!" Pen cried. "Of course I'm thinking of him! But what if he never comes?"

"He'll come," Rose said fiercely. "And you'd best never doubt it!"

23

WIN'S DUGOUT CANOE SLIPPED through the water as silently as the huge terrapin that swam nearby. Spring had settled comfortably over the river. The forest smelled of damp earth and rotting leaves. Dogwood blossoms hovered like fragile butterflies against the green darkness of cypress and pines. Hawks and bald eagles circled overhead. Pen watched as a hawk plummeted to the water's surface and snatched up a fish—only to have an eagle swoop down and grab the fish away.

"How unfair!" Pen exclaimed. "The poor hawk did all the work, and now he has nothing."

"There's plenty for both," Win said placidly.

"Rose, look at that ugly bird across the river," Pen said.

"It's a pelican," Win told her. "You wouldn't know it to look at him standing there, but when he flies, he's as graceful as a cloud."

Rose was hunched low in the dugout and didn't respond.

"Here we are," Win said.

He rowed to a dock. Pen started to gather up their bundles of clothing and Win leaped out to tie up the canoe.

He helped Pen to the dock, then extended his hand to Rose. Ignoring the gesture, Rose climbed out of the canoe by herself. She brushed past them and started up the path that had been cleared through the trees.

Amity was on her hands and knees in the garden at the side of the house. When she saw them, she stood and wiped her hands on her apron. She hugged Win, then Rose and Pen. Rose stiffened and moved away. Amity's smile flickered, then steadied itself.

"Come in," Amity said. "Supper's almost ready."

The house had a main room with a fireplace for cooking and a bedchamber in back. A ladder led up to the loft.

"You girls will sleep up there," Amity said, pointing to the loft. "But let's have supper before you settle in."

Pen dropped her bundles and went to the hearth, where a pot was bubbling. She picked up a spoon to stir.

"No work for you tonight," Amity said. "This is your welcome-home supper."

She steered Pen to the table. "Sit," she said. "You, too, Rose."

Rose sat down on the bench beside Pen. "Why did you bring us here," Rose asked crossly, "if you don't expect us to work?"

"Oh, you'll work," Amity said. "If you decide to stay.

We'll all have to work if we're to make a go of it."

"What do you mean, *if we decide to stay?*" Rose demanded. "I didn't know we had a choice."

Amity brought a loaf of bread to the table. "You have a choice," she said. "Win and I don't want bonded servants. We need your help, but we want you to stay because you wish to be here."

"We can't pay you at first," Win said, "but you'll have a roof over your heads and full bellies."

"And you're free to leave whenever you like," Amity said.

"And go where, with no money?" Rose demanded.

"If you work hard, we'll pay your passage back to England after we sell our first tobacco," Amity said. "If you want to leave, that is. We hope you won't."

"I'll buy more acreage when we sell the tobacco," Win said. "We'll pay them that helps us with land. You can have something here someday if you're willing to work for it."

Pen felt dazed. Her first thought was that she and Rose didn't deserve this kindness. Not with them planning to run off as soon as they could. But they wouldn't have to run, with Amity and Win offering to pay their passage home—or to give them land if they decided to stay. These people were letting them choose—and them no more than two servant girls that Amity and Win barely knew.

Pen looked up, to find Win watching her. His smile was easy and straightforward, as Pen suspected that Win himself would prove to be. Amity was heaping food on their plates.

"Eat up," Amity said, looking happy. "I don't want one bite to go to waste."

24

A soft May rain was falling when Pen stepped from the house. She paused to look at the herbs and vegetable plants that had sprung up almost overnight in Amity's kitchen garden. Every seed they planted seemed to flourish in the rich loam.

Pen's gaze moved to the tobacco seedlings that stretched from the barn to the edge of the forest. She and Rose had helped Win and Amity with the planting. It had been exhausting work, but Pen watched the plants' steady growth with pride. In late summer, the stalks would be taller than she was, Win said. Then it would be time to cut them to the ground and hang the leaves to cure until early winter. They would store the cured leaves until next summer and then pack them in hogsheads to be shipped to England. If the crop did well, Win would make enough to buy land and to hire more workers. And pay for Pen's and Rose's passage back to England.

Pen walked slowly toward the meadow, enjoying the feel of rain on her face and the sponginess of wet grass beneath her bare feet. The two cows, Bridget and Annie, looked up from their grazing when she approached. Pen patted Bridget's strong neck, then prodded the animals gently on the flanks with a stick. The cows began to move languidly toward home.

They came to the edge of the meadow, where the forest swept in to meet the grazing land. Pen caught a sudden movement in the trees from the corner of her eye. Her heart lurched and she thought, *Indians!* But then the leaves shook and parted, and Bram stepped from the shelter of trees.

"I didn't mean to startle you," he said.

Her heart still pounding, Pen took in the gaunt face, the hollow eyes, the tattered shirt and trousers. He looked terrible!

"It's me," he said, and his voice cracked. He cleared his throat, and then he smiled—or tried to—and Pen started to cry.

She hurried to him and threw her arms around him. She could feel sharp bone and not much meat through his rags. The stench of unwashed flesh filled her nostrils. He sagged against her, as if too weary to stand on his own.

Pen wiped at her eyes. "You need to sit down."

"Aye."

She helped him slide to the ground, where he slumped against a tree.

Pen crouched beside him. "Are you ill?" she asked.

Bram shook his head. "Just tired," he said, "and hungry."

"I'll bring you food."

He reached up to brush the hair from his eyes, and Pen saw that there were bloody wounds around his wrist. She examined his other hand and saw the same ugly cuts. "Did he keep you bound?" she asked in a horrified whisper.

Bram nodded once, quickly, and his jaw tightened.

"How did you get away?"

"He had to take off the irons during the day for us to work," Bram said. "One of the men fell down groaning and holding his belly. While Master Cooper kicked him and accused him of trying to get out of work, I ran. He'll have a party out looking for me by now." Bram's eyes flickered anxiously across the fields. "I have to leave when it gets dark."

"You won't get far without rest," Pen said. "Come with me." With her help, he rose clumsily to his feet. She led him into the cover of trees and raked together a pile of dead leaves and pine needles with her hands. He lay down on the makeshift bed and let out a long sigh.

"For every day I'm gone, it's a week added to my indenture," Bram said. "If I survive the lash."

"They'll have to find you to whip you," Pen said. "Stay here 'til I come back."

"Tell Rose we leave tonight."

"What about Jory and Thomas?" Pen asked.

"I've watched 'em in church and they seem well," Bram said. "From what I hear, they're with good people."

"I've heard the same," Pen responded.

"Then it's you and Rose and me," Bram said. He

157

closed his eyes. "Do you think you could find me something to wear?" he asked through a yawn. "Dressed like this, I'll stand out as a runaway."

"I'll bring you clothing," Pen said. "Just stay hidden and quiet until I come back."

The rain had stopped by the time Pen reached the kitchen yard. Rose was sweeping water from the back steps.

"Bram's here," Pen told her.

Rose's head jerked up. "Truly? He's really come?"

"He's hiding in the woods near the meadow."

"He's not hurt?" Rose asked, frowning. "That man hasn't—"

"Nay, he's just weak," Pen said, "mostly from being half-starved, I'd say. I'm taking him food and clothing. Have Amity and Win come back from Jamestown?"

"Not yet." Rose started up the steps. "I'll see to the food."

Pen found a shirt and trousers of Win's for Bram. When she got back to the kitchen, Rose was filling a basket with bread and cheese.

"Did he say when we'd leave?" Rose asked.

"Tonight." Pen stared at the clothing in her hands. "I hate to steal from Win."

Rose gave her a sharp look. "Surely he won't begrudge a poor bondsman one of his shirts!"

"I'd best take soap and a pail of water," Pen said. "Bram could do with a wash."

"I'll help you carry it all."

"You should be here when Amity and Win come

back," Pen said. "But the cows need milking."

"All right," Rose said impatiently, "I'll see to them. Just tell Bram we'll meet him at the dock."

"Why the dock?"

"They'll be searching the woods and fields for him," Rose said. "Besides, we can travel faster by water. We'll take Win's dugout."

"But Win needs the dugout."

"More than Bram? Look," Rose said, "we have to get Bram away from here. Win can make himself another canoe."

Bram was sleeping when Pen returned. She touched his shoulder and he jerked awake.

"It's only me," she said.

The fear left his eyes. When he saw the basket of food, he sat up and pulled out the loaf of bread.

Pen sat down and watched Bram devour the food. "Rose thinks we should take Win's dugout," she said.

Bram nodded and swallowed. "Good idea."

"Do you know where we're headed?"

"There's a settlement upriver called Falling Creek," Bram said. "Some of the men there go to the northern colonies to hunt and then bring their pelts back to Jamestown to sell. They can tell us how to go. Mayhap they'll let us travel with 'em."

Pen glanced at the sky. The sun was going down. She stood up and brushed wet leaves and twigs from her skirt. "Amity and Win are due back anytime now," she said. "I'd best go before they miss me."

Bram was watching her face. "These people—they've

been good to you? Aye, I can see that for meself. And yet you're willing to risk everything to take off with me."

He lay back in the bed of leaves, looking as if he could sleep again. "You won't be sorry," he said, already closing his eyes.

"Stay here 'til it's time to go to the dock," Pen said gently. "We'll meet you there after everyone's abed."

25

AMITY WAS PUTTING AWAY the food and supplies they had brought from Jamestown when Pen got back to the house.

"Look what Win bought me," Amity said. She pointed to the new kettle on the hearth. "And we brought something for you girls," she added gaily. "Come and see."

Rose glanced up from the bread she was slicing, then dropped her eyes. Pen didn't move from the door.

Amity held out her hand. Crimson-colored ribbons spilled through her fingers. "I thought the color was beautiful," she said, looking expectantly from Pen to Rose.

Pen stared at the ribbons. Yes, they were beautiful. But how could she accept a gift from Amity and Win when she had already stolen from them—and planned to steal more?

"Don't be bashful," Amity said, misinterpreting their hesitancy. "You girls work hard. You deserve a surprise."

Even Rose seemed uneasy when Amity pressed the

ribbon into her hand. She and Pen murmured their thanks, then busied themselves with serving supper. While they ate, Amity talked about everything she and Win had seen in Jamestown. From time to time, she would pause and glance at Pen or Rose, as if waiting for them to fill the silence. When they didn't, Amity would look puzzled, but she didn't question them.

After Amity and Win had gone to bed, Pen and Rose climbed the ladder to the loft. Rose opened a sack she had brought from downstairs. "Bread, salt pork, smoked fish, cheese." She listed the items with satisfaction. "This should keep us fed for a while."

Pen removed her few garments from pegs on the wall and began to roll them up in the blanket from her pallet.

Rose had been watching her. "What's wrong?" Rose demanded. "You're feeling guilty, aren't you? Well, you shouldn't! You've earned this little bit. Besides, Mouse, we're saving 'em the cost of our passage home."

Pen looked up when Rose called her "Mouse." Rose hadn't used that name for a long time, not since they had sailed for Virginia. It reminded Pen of the first time she had seen Rose, strutting down the street in her black-and-crimson gown. Pen smiled, remembering. Then her eyes fell on the hair ribbon and her smile faded.

"I know you're fond of 'em," Rose said. "And I'll admit they're not a bad sort. But we don't belong here. England's home."

Pen nodded quickly and went back to rolling up her

blanket. "I just wish I could tell Amity good-bye, that's all."

"Well, you can't," Rose said bluntly. "You'd only be putting Bram in danger."

"Amity and Win wouldn't turn him in."

"Whether they would or not, you can't say a word."

When they left the house, Pen saw the moon floating high above the river. It had been more than a year since Mam had died, a year since Pen had run away, not knowing what lay in store for her. Now she was running again, and facing the same uncertainties. The wheel of the moon had come full circle.

Bram was waiting at the dock. Rose ran the last few steps and hugged him. Pen couldn't see her face, but she heard Rose sigh. No matter what hardships lay ahead, Pen knew that Rose was content.

Bram lowered himself into the dugout, then took their bundles and helped Rose into the canoe. Rose looked up at Pen, waiting.

Pen didn't move.

"We should leave right away," Bram said to Pen, "and be far away by first light. Don't be afraid."

"It's not fear that's stopping her," Rose said.

"Pen—listen." Bram's voice had grown sharp. "No matter how good they've been to you, you're still just a servant here."

"I don't feel like a servant," Pen said. And it was true. Amity and Win weren't her masters; they were her friends. But so was Bram. And he needed her. How could

163

she turn her back on him now? And yet—how could she go? Pen had expected nothing but pain and loneliness in Virginia. Mayhap even death. What she had found instead was a family. It was something she had wanted so much—and had been so certain she would never have again—she hadn't even dared wish for it. And now, it was hers. All she had to do was accept it. Mam would understand, Pen thought. Nay—more than that!—Mam would rejoice.

"I can't go with you," Pen said.

"Of course you can go!" Bram cried.

The canoe rocked as Rose reached out her hand. Pen stooped to take it. "Don't worry, Mouse," Rose said, and Pen could hear a touch of the old sass in Rose's voice. "I'll take care of him."

"I know you will," Pen said. "And take care of yourself."

"We need you, Pen." Bram sounded hurt and bewildered.

"Nay," Pen said, "you and Rose have all you need."

This was the truth, and it brought Pen comfort. But Pen knew that she would miss Bram for a very long time. Mayhap the memory of this splendid fair-haired boy would always be bittersweet, would forever cause a tender ache in her heart. Only time could answer that.

Pen gripped Rose's hand until the dugout began to move away from the dock.

"Godspeed," she called after them.

She watched the canoe until it was lost in the darkness. For a while, she could hear the oars slapping against the water. The sound grew softer and softer, until it was gone.

Only then did Pen turn and start up the hill. The light from the moon had transformed the stones on the path to silver. She followed them home.

AFTERWORD

FROM 1615 TO 1775, at least fifty thousand men, women, and children were transported involuntarily to America. No one knows how many of them were minors. The practice of abducting children off city streets was so prevalent, and treated with such nonchalance, that names and numbers were rarely recorded. Certainly thousands of children were kidnapped from the British Isles during the seventeenth and eighteenth centuries. In August of 1627 alone, at least fourteen hundred English children and young adults were captured by spirits and transported to Virginia. Their ages ranged from five to seventeen.